Born in 1962, Melbourne, Victoria, the author has lived on a small island in South East Queensland, Australia, since 2007. She lived and worked in Sweden for five years and graduated in Utah, U.S.A. A qualified counsellor and life coach, the author worked with young school students from diverse backgrounds and specialised conditions for eight years. During this time she worked with 'Closing the Gap' alongside her friend Leonie Watson, Elder of the Muandik People, helping Aboriginal and Torres Strait Islander school students learn more about their culture.

The author wrote her first unpublished children's book at the age of 17 years winning an 'Alpha Betta Gamma' award.

The illustrator, Sallie-Anne Swift is an award winning Australian artist living in Long Beach California and sister of the author.

Sallie-Anne also illustrated the first novel of the *Mangrove Sands* series.

This book is dedicated to Ethel Watson, the last Queen of the Muandik People, Kingston, South Australia. Ethel lived for most of her life at Blackford Reserve. She was the last full blood Aboriginal in the SE who died in 1954, at age of 80 years, from influenza in the Kingston Hospital. A memorial was erected in 1971 by the Kingston Branch of the National Trust at the town's entrance and the first memorial dedicated to an Aboriginal person in South Australia. A portrait of Ethel Watson hangs in the Adelaide Museum.

L. J. Nilsson

MANGROVE SANDS, THE ENCHANTED SEAWORLD AND BEYOND

Illustrated by
Sallie-Anne Swift

AUSTIN MACAULEY PUBLISHERS™
LONDON • CAMBRIDGE • NEW YORK • SHARJAH

A CIP catalogue record for this title is available from the British
Library.

ISBN 9781398406612 (Paperback)
ISBN 9781398407152 (ePub e-book)

www.austinmacauley.com

First Published 2022
Austin Macauley Publishers Ltd®
1 Canada Square
Canary Wharf
London
E14 5AA

I would like to acknowledge and pay respects to the descendants of Queen Ethel and the Muandik People of Kingston, South Australia, traditional custodians of the land, culture and language referenced in this book and to pay respects to the elders past, present and future.

Respect is further extended to the Australian Aboriginal People and Torres Straight Islanders language, culture, history and perspectives.

Personal thanks are extended to my very good friend, Leonie Joy Lymbery-Watson (Wanjee), Elder of the Muandik People of Kingston, South Australia and direct descendant of Queen Ethel Watson. Your direct support, helpful assistance and knowledge of your Muandik language and culture is greatly appreciated. A wonderful example of the collaboration of two cultures working together with the same perspective, ultimately to help others (children) learn, understand and respect cultural diversity and inclusion.

All research has been conducted with the inclusion and written permission from the Muandik people and in accordance with the United Nations Declaration the rights of indigenous people, including principles of indigenous rights to self-determination and to full participation in developments that impact on their lives.

Synopsis

A sequel to Mangrove Sands, The Enchanted Seaworld. This book includes the same Characters with the inclusion of a ten-year-old aboriginal girl, 'Wanjee', with a focus on educating both indigenous and non-indigenous children about aboriginal language, culture and dream time stories, in particular, the Muandik tribe located in Kingston, South Australia.

Special written permission to reference the Moandik language, dream time stories and symbolic art has been obtained from the Muandik elders and direct descendants of Queen Ethal from the Moandik tribe, Kingston, South Australia.

The sequel sets out to inspire and educate children who, for one reason or another, have difficult starts in life either by fate or disability. Each chapter provides a human lesson and human qualities through adventure including; Empathy, bravery, initiative, honour, friendship and resilience in the face of adversity. The sequel aims to promote cultural diversity and inclusion and provide hope and a sense of belonging through a magical underwater sea world of talking animals and friendship.

Through adventure and mishap, the children learn many lessons from their enchanted Seaworld mentors and friends, including responsibility, how to handle bullies at school through philanthropist techniques, encouraging goals and aspirations, environmental awareness, true friendship and the power of forgiveness.

With a focus on the aboriginal Muandik language and culture, Wanjee is chosen to come to the Enchanted Seaworld away from her foster parents who are not very nice. She teaches her friends the art of making a boomerang, a didgeridoo, language from her culture, symbolic aboriginal art, several dream time stories, bush medicine for healing wounds and cultural celebrations.

The children all do very well at school thanks to the tutoring from their enchanted Seaworld friends. They all go on to win awards and are celebrated for their human qualities highlighting that one means nothing without the other.

Finally, Wanjee returns to her family on South Seabrook island, Maria and Tommy transition to high school and they all look forward to a new and exciting, epic journey.

Proposed: Book 3 Mangrove Sands, The Enchanted Seaworld

The Epic Journey

Introduction

On a small island located in South East Queensland, Australia, four children, Dino, Tommy, Maria and Jake, have difficult starts in life and are offered a better life by Parlow the Pelican. They are given a magical seaweed necklace with a gold ingot and a secret code of silence written on it. The children must wear this ingot in order to enter the Enchanted Sea World that lies beneath Mangrove Sands. They enter this magical world through a tunnel dug out by soldier crabs where they discover a magical new world where all the animals can talk and soon become the children's mentors, friends and family.

Every Friday evening the children are collected by Parlow and tutored by the Dugongs, Wally, Delilah and Pedro. They enjoy many adventures and mishaps including; nearly drowning in Ollie octopus cave, learning how to capture octopus, being saved from a bull shark ride, fun times on the Seaweed Slide, operated by Mut and Tut turtle, Johanna's Ferris wheel ride and enjoying delicious food and treats made by Ibis Chef.

They learn many human lessons and by the end of the year have transitioned from failing students to the top of their class.

The children break up for the Christmas school holidays and Dino leaves with his sick mother to attend high school on the mainland. When Tommy, Maria and Jake return back to the island from their holidays they discover a terrible thing has happened to Jake's gold ingot.

Chapter 1

The Missing Ingot

It was a warm Thursday afternoon in January 2019, the school holidays were almost over before it was time to start a new school year.

The children had all spent their holidays off the island and were looking forward to seeing each other and visiting the Enchanted Sea World again.

When Jake arrived home from his holiday on the Gold Coast, he was excited about seeing his friends and visiting the Enchanted Sea World the following night.

But when he went to his cupboard to check his ingot in his old sand shoe, he was horrified to discover the shoes were gone.

"Grandpa, Grandpa?" yelled Jake in a panicked voice. Grandpa walked up the hallway, slowly limping on one leg as if every bone in his body ached.

"What's all the yelling about?" inquired Grandpa.

"Where are my old sand shoes?" Jake asked desperately.

"What? Those old things! I threw them out while you were on holidays," Grandpa replied.

Jake raced outside to the green council bins, pulling everything out in a panic.

"That's no use," said Grandpa as he watched Jake. "The Garbo's collected the bins several times over the holidays," he said quite casually.

"OH NO! They are my lucky shoes, I have to find them," said Jake in desperation.

"Good luck with that," replied Grandpa with a giggle.

Jake was in a panic, his mind was racing; wondering how was he going to find his shoes and the gold ingot? He would never get back into the Enchanted Sea World without it.

He quickly grabbed his bike and told grandpa he was going to see if Maria and Tommy were back from their holidays.

Jake's mind was racing as he rode his bike. His mind was jumping from one question to the next; the shoes would be at the tip, probably under tons and tons of rubbish. How would they get there? How would they find the shoes? Would they be allowed into the tip? Would the ingot still be in the shoe? The more Jake felt panicked by all his thoughts, the more the sweat ran down his face and his hands perspired.

As he sped into Tommy's driveway, a cloud of red dust sprayed up behind him as he came to a screeching halt.

Tommy came out onto his porch waving. "Hey Jake, how are you man?" he inquired with a broad smile, pleased to see his friend.

Jake jumped off his bike, ran up to Tommy, threw his arms around him and patted him quickly on the back saying, "Hi man, good to see you. I have a serious problem. Grandpa threw my shoes out into the garbage while I was away, you know the one's I mean, my secret shoes."

"Okay, okay, slow down, come into my room," replied Tommy who knew this was serious. If they couldn't find the ingot, Jake would never get back to the Enchanted Sea World.

Tommy had only arrived home one hour before Jake came tearing into the driveway like a whirling tornado. "I'll get you some water, you sure are sweaty," said Tommy as they entered his bedroom.

"What are we going to do?" asked Jake nervously, sitting on the edge of Tommy's bed.

Tommy handed Jake a cold glass of water and slowly walked around his room, hand on his head, deep in thought, when he suddenly stopped and shouted, "I've got it! I know what we will do!" said Tommy.

"What? What?" said Jake excitedly, bouncing on the end of Tommy's bed almost falling off.

"Where do they take our garbage to?" Tommy queried.

"To the tip at Junkyard Well opposite South Seabrooke island," replied Jake.

"That's right and who has the best pair of eyes from the sky and comes from the Enchanted Sea World?" Tommy asked.

"Shian! Shian! The whistling Kite. He can find the shoes," yelled Jake excitedly.

"Yes, exactly," replied Tommy with a smile. "Unfortunately, you will have to stay home tomorrow while Maria and I go to the Enchanted Sea World until we find your ingot," said Tommy with a more serious tone.

Jake looked disappointed as he nodded his head, but was happy they had a plan to find his lost ingot.

"We must go and see if Maria is home and explain the whole thing to her," said Jake.

Jake was feeling relieved, now they had a plan; he had restored hope of finding his lost ingot. As he was feeling more relaxed, his thoughts turned to his friends. "Hey, it's strange without Dino here. Did you hear from him over the holidays?" inquired Jake.

"Yeah, he called me and said it was taking him a while to settle in, that his mum was being well cared for and he missed all of us," replied Tommy.

"Wish he was here," replied Jake forlornly.

The boys grabbed their bikes and began riding over to Maria's house, chatting about what they did over the holidays. Jake had spent most of his time surfing on the Gold Coast with his older brother who lived there with his wife. Tommy spent his holidays on a cattle farm in Tamworth with his grandfather, mustering cattle, shearing sheep and fishing by the lake almost every day.

As the two boys pulled up in Maria's driveway, she ran down her front stairs with a big smile and hugged both the boys. "I never want to walk my Auntie's Chihuahua EVER AGAIN," protested Maria, and they all laughed together as Maria always stayed with her Auntie on the Sunshine Coast and always had to walk her Auntie's yappy, Chihuahua.

"C'mon guys, let's ride to the treehouse to catch up; we have something to tell you, Maria," said Tommy.

"I'll just get my bike," replied Maria who ran to the shed at the back of her house and pulled out her bike. She sped to the front and they all rode off swiftly towards their cubby house at Mangrove Sands.

Riding through the red dirt tracks lined with Gum trees, the cool afternoon breeze swept across their faces. Jake took his usual shortcut trying to beat Tommy and Maria to the cubby house. When Tommy and Maria saw Jake take off and yell, "Beat you there," they all sped up and the race was on! Maria screaming out to Tommy in front, "Go, Tommy, go." Just as Tommy and Maria turned the corner to the cubby house, Jake sped out of the bush in front of them shooting a cloud of red dust into their faces.

"Beat you again guys," said Jake as Tommy and Maria wiped red dust off their faces. Jake laughed at the sight of Tommy and Maria's red faces.

"You'll keep doing that," said Tommy laughing.

As they climbed up the rope ladder to the treehouse, Maria was telling the boys how good it was to be back. "It's so much more fun here than at my Auntie's. I hope I get to stay here on the island next holidays."

As they all sat down in the cubby house, Maria began asking the boys about their holiday but Tommy had more important things to discuss. "I'll tell you later, first, I must tell you what has happened," said Tommy quite concerned.

"What? What?" replied Maria in an anxious tone.

"Quite simply, while Jake was away on holidays on the Gold Coast, his grandfather had a cleanout and threw Jake's sandshoes into the garbage bin, the one's with his ingot in them," said Tommy.

"Oh no, what are we going to do? This is dreadful," said Maria aghast.

"Yes, I know," replied Tommy. "I have come up with a plan. No doubt the shoes are at the tip with everyone else's rubbish, possibly buried under a lot of rubbish now. We will ask Shian the Whistling Kite, who can see the tiniest speck with his sharp radar eye sight from the sky, to help us find it."

"That's a great idea," replied Maria. "But how will Jake get to the Enchanted Sea World tomorrow night, without his ingot?" replied a confused Maria.

"Maybe I could use Dino's ingot," suggested Jake with excitement.

"Do you recall Parlow telling us before the holiday that a new girl, 'Wanjee' is supposed to be coming to the Enchanted Sea World for the first time? And she will be using Dino's ingot?"

"Oh that's right," replied Maria.

"Jake will need to stay at home tomorrow, it will just be you, me and Wanjee." Tommy answered pointing to Maria and himself. Jake looked disappointed but knew he had no other choice but to stay at home and allow his friends to look for his ingot.

After the children had spent some time discussing their plan to find Jake's ingot and telling one another about their holiday adventures, several hours had passed and the children decided they needed to go home, unpack and get all their things ready for school the following day.

"I still have to cover all my books," exclaimed Maria.

"I have to find my school clothes and make sure I have all my books ready, it's a big year this year. It's the last year of Primary school for us," said Tommy as he nudged Maria.

"Yeah," said Jake looking a little glum. "I'll be left here on my own when you go to high school next year," replied Jake.

"Don't worry, Jake, you will have the new girl and your Enchanted Sea World family, and it's a whole year away," assured Tommy.

The children rode off towards their homes, waving goodbye to each other and calling out, "See ya tomorrow at school, guys."

"Bye."

"Tomorrow." Followed by a thumbs up.

It was a warm Friday morning, the children were eager to get to school, meet their new teachers and start another new year. The new girl whose name was Wanjee was in Jake's class but she did not know the plans that awaited her in the Enchanted Sea World and the children kept quiet about it. When the bell rang for the end of the first day of school, the children met on their bikes and were excited as they would see their Enchanted Sea World family in the evening and Wanjee would meet the Enchanted Sea World for the very first time.

They took off on their bikes racing each other down the hill, as they did every day after school until they arrived at Jake's street. Jake wished Maria and Tommy good luck finding his ingot before riding home with a feeling of disappointment at not being able to join them. "I will miss coming with you tonight, but I hope you can find my ingot," said Jake, breathing heavily from racing his friends down the hill.

"We will miss having you with us, but we will do everything to find your ingot, mate," replied Tommy.

Tommy and Maria were excited to be reuniting with their Enchanted Sea World friends and eager to complete all their tasks at home before their evening adventure. In excited anticipation, both Maria and Tommy found their ingots where they had secretly hidden them and went to bed early.

That evening, Jake lay in his bed imagining Maria, Tommy and Wanjee in the Enchanted Sea World. How he longed to see his Dugong tutors, Wally, Delilah and Pedro. He wondered how Cane the "Yellow Crested Cockatoo" was, how big Ollie octopus babies had grown and giggled silently when he thought of Cram the crab and how his food talked after they ate the delicious Enchanted Sea World fruits. Jake finally fell asleep, hoping that Shian the Sea Eagle would find his ingot so he could visit the Enchanted Sea World next week.

Meanwhile, as Tommy lay in bed, holding his ingot with his eyes half-closed he heard the familiar 'swoosh, thud!' sound of Parlow landing on his window sill. Tommy sat up, eyes wide open with a big broad smile stretched from one ear to the other when he saw Parlow on his window sill.

Tommy quietly opened the window and gave Parlow a huge hug. "Sh-hello, son," said Parlow affectionately.

"Oh, I missed you, Parlow," said Tommy warmly.

As Tommy was about to tell Parlow about Jake's lost ingot, Parlow said, "Sh-sh-sh-I know, son and I have brought Dino's ingot for Jake."

"What about Wanjee?" inquired Tommy.

"She will come with us next week," replied Parlow.

"Oh wow, Jake is going to be so excited," said Tommy as he lay back in bed rubbing his ingot and repeating the code of silence. He raised up, out of his body still lying in his bed and like a floating feather, landed on Parlow's soft, feathery, white back. Once again enjoying the feeling of Parlow's silky feathers through his fingers and touching the side of his face as Parlow ascended up into the sky towards Maria's house.

As they began descending towards Maria's house, Tommy could clearly see Maria's face in the moonlight, pressed up against the window sill with her big broad smile.

She quickly opened her window and gave Parlow a huge affectionate hug. "My lovely Parlow, it is so good to see you," Maria said with joy.

"Sh-it's lovely to see sh-you again too," replied Parlow.

Maria quickly lay back in bed, held her ingot and eagerly repeated the code of silence. As she floated onto Parlow's white feathery back Tommy explained that they were picking up Jake, that he would use Dino's ingot. Maria was even more excited that the three of them would be returning to the Enchanted Sea World together.

Parlow descended onto Jake's window sill but Jake was sound asleep. He had no idea he would be going with them tonight. Parlow tapped his beak on Jake's window. Jake yawned and slowly opened one eye. When he saw Parlow, Maria and Tommy he sat up excitedly, loudly whispering as he opened the window, "Parlow, Parlow, Parlow, I didn't think I would be going tonight, oh it's good to see you." Jack hugged his feathery white friend.

"Sh-here," said Parlow, "take Dino's ingot. Parlow opened his large protruding pelican beak and inside was Dino's ingot. Jake grabbed the ingot and lay back in bed, quickly repeating the code of silence and floating onto Parlow's back behind Maria and Tommy.

"Sh-hold on tight," said Parlow, flying off the windowsill, souring high up over the island towards Mangrove Sands.

A warm summer evening breeze swept over the children's faces, and the sky glittered with shining bright stars. The cicadas were singing with their translucent wings as the three children excitedly flew towards their happy place.

After they landed at Mangrove Sands, next to a large stingray hole, Parlow did his soldier crab call, "EEEEEEEE" and thousands of soldier crabs began digging as the mangrove seeds lined the walls of the tunnel.

One by one, Tommy, Maria and Jake repeated the code of silence and at the speed of light, they shot down the tunnel like a rocket bumping into the closed door at the bottom.

"Stand back Parlow is coming," shouted Tommy. Just as the children stepped aside, Parlow came hurtling down the tunnel, thumping into the door, feathers flying everywhere. "Oh, dear," said Parlow shaking himself off, "I sh-must put a pillow back sh-on that door." The children giggled as they brushed Parlow's white feathers off themselves.

Once again, the tunnel door opened and in shone a beam of rainbow light. The children followed Parlow walking up the golden winding path, as they had done so many times before, towards the jewel coated Clam Castle.

Halfway along the path the children heard a familiar loud, shrill sound as Cane flapped his white feathers and bobbed his yellow-crested head excited to see the children again.

"Wha-hallo, hallo, hallo," he squawked to each of the children.

"Hello, Cane you funny cockatoo, how nice to see you again," said Maria with a giggle. Cane perched himself on Maria's shoulder bobbing his head in delight.

As they neared the castle, Jake was still puzzled, how did Parlow know about his lost ingot?

"Parlow?" Jake inquired, "How did you know I had lost my ingot?"

"Oh Jake, you should know by now that Parlow knows everything," replied Tommy.

Once they arrived at the castle's entrance, Parlow stood facing the children, spreading his wings out and standing straight and tall to gain the children's attention.

"I will let sh-you in on a little secret," said Parlow. "When sh-you think I am sh-sleeping, I am not. In my mind's eye I can see sh-all that you do, feel and sh-say," Parlow announced. The children looked astonished.

"So when we see you with your eyes closed, you're not really sleeping, but watching us?" questioned Jake.

"Sh-that's right," replied Parlow with a grin.

"That is soooo cool," said Tommy rather impressed with Parlow's abilities.

"You're just like our guardian angel," Maria said warmly.

"You could say that. Sh-c'mon kids, time to say good morning to sh-your tutors. We will discuss finding the missing ingot in sh-class," said Parlow walking through the castle's jewel covered entrance.

Excitedly, the children entered the castle, walking past the dining area where they said hello to Ibis Chef who was preparing an assortment of delicious fresh food. He nodded his head at the children as he sliced fresh watermelon with his long black beak. Jake put his hand out to take a piece of watermelon off the plate. "UH, UH, UH." Ibis fiercely nodded his head to the left and right looking sternly at the children.

The children laughed and made their way down the pearl slate corridor and through the red ruby door into their classroom. Their clam shell desks stood facing the pool exactly as they had left them before the holidays. Suddenly, a large bald head emerged from the pool. The children raced over to the edge of the pool to greet their master teacher Wally. Maria put her face against Wally's wet skin. "Oh, Wally, I have missed you," said Maria affectionately.

"Ditto," replied Tommy and Jake.

More water sprayed up out of the pool and Delilah with her bright pink spectacles and Pedro emerged. "Hello children," splattered Delilah.

The children were delighted to see their tutors again who had encouraged and taught them so many life lessons last year and become their supportive sea world family.

"Right children, take a seat sh-at your desks," said Parlow with an official tone.

"Wally, would you please transfer the map onto the virtual screen?" Wally visualised the map and there it was on the virtual screen elevated above the children.

The children all stared in astonishment. There on the screen was a map of the local tip located on a nearby island called 'Junkyard Well'. A large red cross marked the location of the ingot, right in the middle of Junkyard Well.

"But how did you know?" questioned Jake.

"I have a sixth sh-sense to danger and sh-saw your grandfather throw sh-your sandshoes in the bin, I followed the garbage sh-truck and watched where sh-they dumped the rubbish."

"Why didn't you go and get the ingot?" queried Jake.

"Because sh-son, that is sh-your responsibility," answered Parlow. Jake lowered his head and nodded in agreement.

At that moment, a swoosh of air passed over Jake's face.

"Shian!" The children all squealed in excitement as the whistling kite landed on the edge of the pool.

"Listen up children, sh-you will all take sh-your carts and follow Shian to Ollie's cave, he sh-will be waiting for you," instructed Parlow.

"No class today?" questioned Tommy.

"No son, not th-all lessons th-are conducted in the classroom," replied Wally with a knowing smile.

The children were eager to start their adventure and catch up with their other enchanted friends. One by one, they thanked their tutors and with Shian flying ahead, made their way outside to their clam cladded carts.

With Shian soaring high in front of the children, they drove their carts towards Ollie's cave. The grass was bright emerald green, fresh pawpaws, bananas and vegetables surrounded them in abundance. "Squawk, squawk," Cane said as he landed on the side of Maria's cart and passed her half a juicy mango he had sliced with his beak, just as he had done on their very first visit to the Enchanted Sea World.

"Thank you, my feathery friend," said Maria biting into the juicy mango.

"Oh look," announced Tommy, "there's Joanna at the Ferris wheel." The children waved and shouted hello to their friend, Joanna Goanna who was sunning herself in a deck chair beside the Ferris wheel. Joanna gave the children a wave and they proceeded towards the 2 km water slide where Mut and Tut turtle were sitting. The children waved at their friends as they continued towards Ollie's cave, driving their carts slowly up the steep hill.

Once they reached the top of the hill, they soon realised the carts wouldn't make it down the rocky descent. "We will never get the carts down this rocky hill. Just park them next to the eucalyptus trees and we'll walk down," instructed Tommy.

Shian was waiting on the top of Ollie's cave as the children carefully began descending down the rugged rock face. They could see Ollie at the mouth of the cave with his babies, Harry, Larry and Mow beside him.

"Be careful," called out Ollie as he extended his long tentacle arm for them to hold onto as they climbed over the last few rocks to the bottom.

"High five," Harry spluttered, slapping his slimy tentacle arm onto Tommy's arm.

Tommy giggled and squirmed, "You guys sure are slimy and you've grown since we last saw you."

"Bigger and cheekier," replied Ollie with a sense of pride.

Shian let out a loud screech as a sign to keep going.

"Let's go kids," said Ollie as he led the children through the tunnel towards South Seabrooke Island. Shian flew ahead as the children made their way through the cave, past their favourite water pool full of exotic corals and brightly coloured fish life until they saw the light at the end of the cave.

As the children followed Shian towards the Southern end of South Seabrooke Island, Ollie and the babies swam in the shallow water beside them. Once they reached the tip of the island, the children could clearly see 'Junkyard Well' lying approximately 1km across the ocean from South Seabrooke Island.

Shian let out an ear-piercing call. Suddenly, three of the biggest whistling kites, which looked more like gyrocopters, flew above them with double braided anchor ropes attached to either side of their legs secured to a flat plank of wood.

"Hold your arms up and bend your knees," instructed Shian to the children.

The kites approached the children from behind, as the children stood with their arms up in the air Maria called out, "Look the kites have swing's attached to their legs."

Then a plank of wood hit their bottoms and they each grabbed the ropes. Within seconds all three children were flying on swings beneath three giant Whistling Kites, soaring only metres above the ocean.

"C'mon ph-kids," said Ollie to his children, "we will swim across quickly ph-and meet them ph-over at Junkyard Well."

As the kites approached 'Junkyard Well' they began to ascend, climbing higher to the top of the Well, then gradually but carefully lowering the children until their feet touched the ground and they could stand up.

What the children saw within the well made them feel sick to their stomachs. "Ah, yuck! Yuck! Yuck!" Jake repeated as he turned away from the Well full of stenchy water filled with rubbish and waste including; plastic, food, clothing, fridges, metals, oils and an assortment of discarded waste.

"How on earth will we ever find my ingot in that stinky, toxic well?" proclaimed a dejected Jake.

"Don't ph-worry Jake, we will ph-find your ingot," said Ollie as five slimy heads appeared over the cliff.

"Wow, you guys can climb over land, that's awesome," said Jake impressed.

"Look over there in the middle of the well." Tommy pointed at Shian who was hovering over the same location which was marked with a red cross on the map in class this morning.

"It must be in there somewhere," said Jake with slightly more enthusiasm.

By now, Shian was swooping vertically up and down indicating the spot just above the waste, in the middle of the well.

Jake was at the edge of the well, looking hesitant to venture into the filth, "We ph-will get it ph-for you," announced Ollie. "C'mon kids," said Ollie to his children.

"But ph-Dad, it ph-stinks," protested Larry.

"It will wash ph-off," replied Ollie.

Jake was extremely relieved that he didn't have to go into the well. Harry, Larry, Mow and Pip reluctantly followed their father, slithering over the waste, they made their way to the spot where Shian was swooping.

There was a very large, old rusted fridge on the spot indicated. "C'mon kids, attach your ph-arms to the ph-fridge," instructed Ollie. With all of their 8 arms x 5, a total of 45 tentacled arms were attached to the fridge. "On the count ph-of three," Ollie said. "1, 2, ph-3," and the Octopus threw the fridge off the spot.

"Can you see anything?" yelled Jake.

"Not yet," yelled back Larry.

Under the fridge lay several old rusted lawnmowers. Larry grabbed the bottom of one and just as he went to lift it, the blade underneath cut one of his tentacle arms clean off.

Tommy, Jake and Maria looked on in horror. They were even more horrified to see Harry, Mow and Pip laughing at Larry.

It is a well-known fact that octopus have no bones and have the ability to regrow any part of their bodies within a few weeks if predators damage them, but the children did not know this.

Larry saw the look of horror on the children's faces and yelled back, over his siblings' laughter. "It's ph-okay guys, it will grow back within ph-one week."

The children were relieved and astounded by how clever their octopus friends really were.

Parlow knew exactly where the ingot lay and was sending telepathic messages to Shian. "If you can see an old mattress, the ingot is caught in the spring of the mattress," said Shian.

"There's the ph-mattress, it's under the mower," cried out Pip. Ollie tossed the mower aside with his long tentacled arms uncovering a filthy, torn mattress embedded in filthy slush and putrid water.

The five octopuses used all 45 identical arms (minus 1) and lifted the mattress up, laying it on top of all the filth and waste. They began tearing off what material remained on the mattress until they uncovered the springs.

Jake noticed a round light shining on his shirt. "There it ph-is," cried out Pip. As they moved the mattress the light on Jake's shirt moved, the sun was reflecting the light onto the ingot and it was reflecting the light back onto Jake's shirt.

Carefully, Ollie untied the seaweed necklace that was caught in the spring and threaded it over one of his arms. The octopuses were covered in stench and filth as they glided over the trash towards the children who were waiting patiently on the edge of the Well.

Ollie extended his arm, "Here ph-you go, son," said Ollie. Jake didn't care how filthy the ingot was, he was happy to have his ingot back and quickly took it off Ollie's arm.

"Thank you so much," Jake said appreciatively.

"A messy, ph-but successful mission," replied Ollie, shaking the rotten food and filthy debris off his body.

The giant whistling kite returned with swings hanging from their legs and soared past the children.

"The kar-kites will fly you back to your kar-carts, time is running out and Ibis has food prepared for you," instructed Shian.

Ollie and the children were keen to return to the fresh saltwater and wash themselves. "We will see you all next week," said Ollie as he and the babies began descending down Junkyard Well towards the ocean.

The children could see the kites returning. "Quick, get ready for the swing, here they come," shouted Jake. The children held their arms up ready to grab the ropes.

"Woo-hoo," cried out Maria as she flew up into the sky on her swing, followed by Jake and Tommy. The kites flew across the ocean towards the Enchanted Sea World. "Look down there," called out Tommy to the others. Down below them in the ocean were Ollie, Larry, Harry, Mow and Pip all splashing around taking a well-deserved bath in the ocean.

The kites began to ascend as they flew over Ollie's cave and up the rocky hill face, landing the children gently next to their carts. The children thanked the whistling kites who let out a screech and flew away over the eucalyptus trees.

When the children arrived back at the castle, Parlow was sitting in his grand shell clad chair with his eyes closed. Jake tiptoed up to Parlow's ear and whispered, "You know I found the ingot, don't you?"

Parlow opened one eye and with a knowing smile said, "Yes I do, sh-son."

The children were very hungry after their adventure and after a quick wash of their hands and cleaning the ingot, made their way to the dining table. Ibis Chef had again prepared a feast of delicious food including; passion fruit pies, strawberry and mango smoothies, banana cake, pineapple fritters and salad rolls full of fresh crisp lettuce, juicy red tomatoes and sliced beetroot.

The children had just finished devouring the delicious food when Parlow looked at the clock, it was now 9 pm. "Time to sh-get going," announced Parlow. The children thanked Ibis for the delicious food and as they were getting up from the table they heard a familiar popping sound echoing from the kitchen area.

"Oh no, yuck!" The children all repeated and held their noses.

"It's Cram the crab, his food is talking again," said Tommy.

"Nice to smell you again, Cram," said the children giggling on their way out.

"Oh Cram, sh-you really must learn to control yourself," said Parlow laughing as he followed the children outside.

As Parlow and the children walked down the winding golden path towards the tunnel, Parlow asked them all to make an effort to include Wanjee before and after school during the week. Jake had noticed Wanjee when she started school last year, she was very quiet and sat alone, looking sad and her clothes were torn and dirty. He had mentioned Wanjee to Parlow before the holidays but Parlow seemed to already know about Wanjee and told the children she would take Dino's ingot after the holidays.

"Next Friday sh-will be Wanjee's sh-first visit to the Enchanted Sea World, remember, family can be anyone sh-who is kind and supportive," said Parlow.

The children could see the Humpback Whale at the water's edge. One by one, the children stood in front of the tunnel door waiting for the whale's pressurised water to hit them, shooting them one by one, up the tunnel-like rockets and landing back on Mangrove Sands.

"Oosh," said a wet Tommy, landing in a stingray hole full of muddy water. "I forgot to grab a towel."

When Parlow shot out of the hole, he took one look at the soaked children and knew he was going to get wet. "Next sh-time, bring a towel" said a disgruntled Parlow.

Thankfully, there was a warm northerly wind blowing which was like standing in front of a hairdryer at full speed. By the time Parlow delivered the children home they were all dry.

Jake was the last to be dropped home. "Remember son, hide your ingot in a safe place this time," said Parlow with a smile.

After Parlow had left, Jake looked around his bedroom looking for a safe place to hide his ingot. He recalled a hole in the floorboards under his bed. He found an old shoebox, put the ingot inside and placed it carefully into the hole, covering the hole with some books.

The noise on the floorboards startled grandpa who shuffled down the hallway. Jake heard him coming and jumped quickly into bed just as his doorknob began to turn. "What's going on in here, I thought I heard a rat on the floorboards."

"All good in here Grandpa," replied Jake.

"Hey, did you find your old sandshoes at the tip yesterday?" giggled Grandpa.

"Nah, unfortunately not," replied Jake.

"I don't know why you wanted those scruffy old shoes anyway," said Grandpa.

"Sometimes Grandpa, old things have more meaning than new things," proclaimed Jake.

"Goodnight Grandpa," said Jake closing his eyes.

Chapter 2

Magical Messages

The following day, the children completed their chores and all met up on their bikes, to ride to their cubby house, as they did every Saturday. Tommy went over to Jake's, skidding his bike in the red soil at the front of his house. Jake came out, grabbed his bike and they began riding towards Maria's.

"Hey, did you hide your ingot in a better place?" inquired Tommy. "Yep, it's in a hole in a shoebox, under my bed," replied Jake.

"Good place! Hey! Race ya to Maria's," Tommy said, speeding up his bike and darting through a bush track.

"Hahaha, good luck," shouted Jake who knew all the shortcuts.

Tommy couldn't see Jake as he rode into Maria's driveway at top speed and thought he had finally won until

Jake walked out of the house with Maria. "HAHAHA next time, Tommy." Jake laughed.

They all laughed and had just started to make their way on their bikes towards their cubby at Mangrove Sands when they saw Wanjee sitting by herself on the concrete curb by the edge of the road.

They all stopped and lay their bikes down. Wanjee put her head in to her knees as Maria sat down, slowly next to her. "Hey, are you okay?" Maria asked quietly concerned. Wanjee nodded her head no. "Would you like to come with us to our cubby treehouse?" gestured Maria. Wanjee nodded her head but this time it was a yes.

"C'mon," said Maria, holding her hand out to Wanjee. "You can double dink on my bike."

Wanjee stood up slowly, her jeans were torn, she had no shoes and her long dark curly hair was all matted. "Do you need to tell your parents?" inquired Maria.

"Nup, they don't care where I am," replied Wanjee sadly.

"Jump on the seat, I will peddle standing up," said Maria. Wanjee was a ten-year-old aboriginal girl with long, dark, curly hair, dark brown skin and deep hazel eyes. She was a very tall, thin girl and had only started at the island school two weeks before the end of the school year.

"You're so tall, you can easily touch the ground while I get going," Maria said impressed by Wanjee's height. Wanjee gave her a little smile, balancing the bike with her long legs while Maria started peddling and off they set towards the cubby house at Mangrove sands.

The boys didn't race their bikes as they usually do instead, they slowed down to keep pace with Maria and Wanjee. As they neared the tree house they veered left off the road and down a gradual descent onto a bush track surrounded by bottle brush, tea tree and eucalyptus trees. "There it is," said Maria pointing the cubby out to Wanjee.

They all rested their bikes against the trunk of their tree house, Tommy went up first, then Jake. Maria urged Wanjee to follow the boys up the anchor rope ladder and soon followed behind her.

Once they were inside, Maria explained that the tree house was the place they all came to, to sort things out and discuss anything and everything. "We call that place a "Pina Wali **(1.p 200, 210)**" in our language," replied Wanjee.

"You have your own language?" queried Tommy.

"Yes, there are many aboriginal languages and dialects in Australia." The children were very impressed.

"We have another friend Dino but he went to the mainland to start high school," Maria explained.

Maria could see Wanjee was still a little bit shy so she asked her what her name meant and where she came from. "I've never heard your name before, does it mean something?" questioned Maria.

"Yes it means hungry, my real name is Arial but my grandmother, who was a Queen, always called me Wanjee because I was always hungry," she said and they all laughed.

"I come from an aboriginal tribe called 'Muandik' located in Kingston, South Australia, we relocated to South Seabrooke island last year," replied Wanjee with a smile. "I miss my family," she added, sadly lowering her head.

"But you said they wouldn't miss you?" queried Tommy.

"Oh the people here are not my parents, they are my foster parents and they don't care about me. All they do is drink and argue," replied Wanjee, almost relieved to share her pain with the others. "My parents are both sick and couldn't look after me, so I was re-homed with these people," said Wanjee.

"That is terrible," Maria empathised. The boys shook their heads and agreed. "They should be reported," stated Jake. "Well, you have us now, and let me assure you, life is going to get better," said Maria putting her arm around Wanjee. Wanjee gave them a smile appreciating the support from her new friends.

For the following hour, the children shared their stories, Tommy telling Wanjee how his parents were killed in a car crash when he was young and now he lives with his grandfather. Jake told Wanjee how his parents were neglectful and now he lives with his sick grandfather and Maria told Wanjee how her father always yells and screams at her. "How do you all stay so happy?" queried Wanjee.

Without giving away their Enchanted Sea World secret, Maria said, "We have each other and now you have us," said Maria compassionately. Tommy and Jake nodded in agreement and they all hugged each other.

It was getting late in the day, the children decided it was time to go home. Wanjee felt much happier, now she had made friends who understood and supported her. As they neared Wanjee's street Maria slowed down and stopped. Wanjee got off the bike, thanked the children and started walking home. "I'll check in Grandpa's garage tomorrow, I think we have a spare bike in there," Jake called out to Wanjee.

Wanjee waved goodbye shouting back to the children, "WuWu **(2 p.199),**" meaning goodbye in her language and went home with a big smile on her face.

The children rode home, chatting on the way. "Wanjee could teach us her language, that would be fun," said Maria.

The boys agreed that having a new language could be a lot of fun. When they reached Tommy's house the boys agreed to catch up in the morning to look for a bike for Wanjee in Grandpas garage. Maria had homework to do so would not be joining them.

The following day, Tommy rode over to Jake's house after breakfast and they both made their way into Grandpas garage.

"I'm sure I saw some bicycle handles under all that equipment in the corner a while ago," said Jake. The boys began sorting the mess, old saws, planks of old timber, tyres, gardening tools, tins of paint and a very long, heavy, rusted chain that appeared to be attached to something under an old single bed mattress. They pulled the mattress off the pile of rubbish and lying on the concrete slab was an old rusted bicycle with flat tyres.

"Well, she ain't no picture, but I reckon we can fix her up for Wanjee," said Jake enthusiastically lifting the bike up.

The boys wheeled the rusty old bike out into the backyard near the hose and began washing it. "I think Grandpa has a tyre pump and if we can find some paint we could sand off the rust and give her a paint. Have a look at the tins of paint we moved and see if they are any good," instructed Jake to Tommy who was already taking the lids off the tins of paint with a flat head screwdriver. "Hey, they are good," Tommy said happily. "One red and one white," said Tommy.

"Hey, if we mix the red and white together?"

And Tommy answered, "We will get PINK!"

The boys smiled at each other and enthusiastically began their project.

"We will need to sand the rust off first," said Jake who had watched his grandfather taking rust off steel framed chairs before. The boys found some course sandpaper and began the preparation work by sanding off all the rust before washing and drying the bike.

They found another very large empty paint tin and poured half the white paint into the tin then as Jake stirred the paint, Tommy poured in the red paint until they had a bright pink colour. "That's enough red paint, its pink enough," said Jake. Both the boys laughed at the lovely pink colour they had created.

"I hope Wanjee likes pink," said Tommy laughing.

The boys found some paintbrushes and stood looking puzzled at the bike. "Do you think we should do a design with some of the white paint left over?" queried Tommy.

"Good idea," replied Jake. "Why don't we paint the base of the bike and handle bars pink and put a white stripe on each side?" suggested Jake.

"Perfect," replied Tommy.

The boys lay the bike on an old towel and painted one side pink, the paint dried quickly so they turned it over and painted the other side. They stood back and began laughing. "It is very pink," said Jake giggling. "Let's paint some white stripes down the handle bars and maybe if we paint the seat white," suggested Jake.

"Good idea," replied Tommy. They washed their brushes, Tommy painted the seat while Jake used a steady hand, to paint a thin white stripe down both handle bars.

Both the boys stood back to look at their finished project. "WOW! That looks mad," said Jake.

"I think Wanjee will love it," said Tommy.

"We need to pump the tyres and it's finished," said Jake rather pleased with himself. As Jake was looking for the tyre pump, he came across an old bike helmet that was a little too for him. "Hey, this might fit Wanjee. Let's paint it pink as well," Jake suggested to Tommy. "Great idea," replied Tommy.

By the time the boys had painted the helmet, pumped the tyres and completed restoring the bike a few hours had passed. As the boys were cleaning up they saw Maria ride down into the back garden. "Oh wow, that looks spectacular, it's nicer than my bike," proclaimed Maria, impressed with what the boys had done. "Did you both paint the bike?" she questioned.

"Yes we did, what do you think?" Jake asked proudly.

"You boys have done an amazing job," replied Maria.

"When are you giving it to Wanjee?" questioned Maria.

"Why not now!" answered Jake. The children agreed that they would take the bike to Wanjee's house.

"How will we find which house she lives in?" stated Maria.

"We will find her, we know what street she walked up so we will find her," said a determined Jake.

The children agreed that they would find Wanjee. Jake stood Wanjee's bike up, "You take one handle bar, Tommy and I'll take the other, we can ride with Wanjee's bike in between us," said Jake.

Riding carefully down the main road on the footpath, they were approaching the street that Wanjee had walked up the day before. The boys turned the corner into the street carefully balancing Wanjee's bike as they turned. Maria rode slowly behind the boys.

They had only ridden 20 metres up the road and it didn't take them long to find Wanjee's house from the terrible shouting, screaming and abusive language coming from a house with overgrown grass and bins full to the brim of empty beer cans. "Oh poor Wanjee, that must be where she lives with her foster parents," Maria said sadly. They all slowed their bikes down as the screaming got louder. They walked gradually towards the house.

"You boys stay here behind the trees, I can see Wanjee outside in the garden, crying."

Maria slowly crept over to the long dry grass beside the fence near where Wanjee was sitting sobbing. "Psst, psst," said Maria, trying to gain Wanjee's attention. Wanjee looked up and was surprised but relieved to see Maria crouched down in the long grass. She crept over to Maria as she wiped her tears.

"You cannot stay here, come with us we have something for you," said Maria with a smile. Wanjee agreed and carefully climbed over the fence, keeping a watchful eye on the house as her foster parents kept screaming at each other inside.

Wanjee felt happier now her friends were with her and wiped the remaining tears using her sleeve and gave Maria a smile. Maria grabbed her hand and said, "C'mon, we have a surprise for you." They ran across the dirt road holding hands when Wanjee saw the boys holding a bright pink bike with white stripes.

"Oh wow, you're going to make me cry again," said Wanjee gratefully. The boys smiled and handed Wanjee the bike. "It's all yours now," said Jake feeling a sense of affection and a warm heart that only giving to others can make you feel.

Wanjee was overwhelmed with gratitude and appreciation, "Thank you so much," she said, "you guys really are the best." She jumped on her bike, eager to ride it.

"C'mon let's have a ride to the cubby house," said Jake excitedly.

"To the 'Pina Wali **(3, p.200,210)**'," replied Wanjee with a broad smile.

Tommy, Jake and Maria all repeated loudly. "Off to the Pina Wali!"

"Off to the Pina Wali!"

"Off to the Pina Wali!"

The children sped off down the road and veered off to the left onto the bush track, Jake darted off into the bush taking a shortcut, as he had always done to try and beat the others but this time he was surprised to see Wanjee at the cubby house first. "How did you get here so fast?" questioned Jake at being defeated for the first time.

Wanjee smiled. "This bike is fast and I am light with long legs, I can outrun most kids my age," Wanjee proudly replied.

Although Jake didn't like to be beaten, he was happy that it was Wanjee who had beaten him and gave her a pat on the back. "I guess there's a first time for everyone," replied Jake graciously. Tommy and Maria arrived and started laughing when they saw Wanjee at the cubby first. Jake and Wanjee joined in the laughter and spent the next few hours chatting in their 'Pina Wali'.

The children had a lovely day, particularly Wanjee who thanked her friends once again for the bike before going back to what she termed the house of horrors. "Wait for us at the bus stop near the power station, we can all ride our bikes to school tomorrow."

Maria told Wanjee before leaving to go home. "Okay, 'Wuwu Wingga **(4)**'," said Wanjee standing on her street corner with her pink bike waving goodbye to her friends.

"What does that mean?" questioned Maria.

"Goodbye friends," replied Wanjee with a smile.

Maria attempted to repeat the words "Wuwu Wiga," replied Maria.

Wanjee laughed. "Good try but it's not Wiga its Wingga," laughed Wanjee.

"Okay, I'll keep practising," replied Maria and the children waved goodbye practising the new words all the way home.

Wanjee rode back to her foster parents with a warmth in her heart, she felt accepted and had a sense of deep pride in who she was and where she came from.

Muandik Language Reclamation report Project, November 2012 (2,3,p199), (1,3,4. pp. 200,210)

Chapter 3

Myths and Legends

The following day the children all met on their bikes, as planned outside the power station and rode to school together. They did this every day for the entire week. When Friday arrived Tommy, Jake and Maria were more excited than ever knowing they would be picking up Wanjee with Parlow that evening. They had managed to keep the secret code of silence and hadn't said a word to Wanjee about their magical Enchanted Sea World or Enchanted friends, who they knew she would meet that night.

When the school bell rang at 2.45 pm, the children all met at the school bike racks and started riding home together. They always arrived at Jake's street first and would stop to say goodbye. This time Jake almost let the cat out of the bag and said, "See you to…nigh…morrow," almost slipping up.

Maria rolled her eyes at Jake so Wanjee didn't see and said goodbye.

The three of them rode until they came to Maria's street on the right-hand side of the main road.

"See you soon, Maria," said Wanjee and gave a cheeky wink to Tommy who winked back and said,

"See you soon, Maria," as she walked across the road with her bike. Tommy and Wanjee continued down the main road over several streets until they came to Tommy's street, also located on the right side of the main road. He told Wanjee he would see her soon and walked across the road with his bike.

"Yeah, probably see you tomorrow," replied Wanjee waving goodbye.

Wanjee lived the furthest away, towards the Southern end of the island just past the power station. She rode slowly home knowing she would find her foster parents either drunk, fighting or asleep. When she arrived home she breathed a sigh of relief, both her foster parents had passed out from the alcohol so she quickly made herself some eggs on toast and took it into her bedroom. She was disgusted with how dirty she was and the state of her uniform and quickly took it off and washed it in the bathroom sink, hanging it over a chair near the window.

She had a shower and washed her hair feeling much cleaner and got into her pyjama's.

Wanjee had been living with her foster parents for five months and her sheets had never been washed. "Tomorrow, I will wash these filthy sheets," Maria said in disgust as she threw an old blanket over the bed to lie on and read a book her mother had given her about their tribe, culture and language. She read the book for several hours and was feeling nostalgic. She always had an ache in her heart being away from her family. Every night, she picked up the only photo she had of her real parents and said goodnight to her mother and father. "I hope you are getting better and I can come back home soon," she said to herself with a tear rolling down her cheek.

It was 7 pm when Parlow arrived on Tommy's window sill, right on time. "Hey Parlow, we have had a good week with Wanjee, we even gave her a bike," said Tommy proudly. "You did very well," replied Parlow as Tommy said the code of silence holding his ingot and floating onto Parlow's feathery white back. They picked up Jake, then Maria who just couldn't contain her excitement.

"This is going to be so much fun," Maria squealed, floating onto Parlow's back behind Jake and Tommy.

Parlow took off into the sky, descending as they passed over the power station until landing on Wanjee's window sill. The children sat on Parlow's back peering in at Wanjee fast asleep. Parlow tapped his long protruding beak on the window which startled Wanjee, she sat up with her eyes wide open in complete surprise. She wiped her eyes, thinking she was dreaming and opened her window. Parlow introduced himself, "Sh-hallo Wanjee, I sh-am Parlow and sh-you know these three on my sh-back. Would sh-you like to come with sh-us and have a better life?" questioned Parlow.

The first thing that came out of Wanjee's mouth is, "You can talk, you're an animal but you can talk," she said, completely overwhelmed by it all.

"Yes sh-dear, I can talk," replied Parlow gently.

"It's okay Wanjee, we couldn't tell you at school. We must all keep a code of silence about all this," said Maria reassuring Wanjee.

Parlow handed Dino's ingot to Wanjee. "Take this, sh-hold it in your hands and sh-read the words on the sh-edge of the ingot." Wanjee took the gold ingot, still unsure if she was dreaming or if all this was real. She was good with languages and didn't have trouble reading the words inscribed on the ingot. "Shamang, Shamoose, Kabang, Kaboose, ziiiiip, shhhhhhhh," she began elevating into the air and out of her body.

"Float over behind me onto Parlow's back," said Maria.

Wanjee couldn't believe what was happening but did as Maria had asked. Maria turned her head around with a big smile and said, "It is okay, Wanjee, now hold onto me tightly."

Parlow flew off the window sill, his wings spread out, as he soared up into the moonlit night sky towards Mangrove Sands.

Wanjee still couldn't believe she was flying with her friends on a talking Pelican but was enjoying the sense of flight and freedom with the night air blowing her long brown curly hair behind her.

Parlow began to descend towards Mangrove Sands and landed, bottom first, next to a large stingray hole. Wanjee had such long legs that when Parlow landed, her knees bent up so high nearly reaching her head and she nearly fell off.

"Hahaha, maybe you should go in front next time," said Maria.

The children climbed off Parlow and he called the soldier crabs and mangrove seeds, "EEEEEEEE."

Wanjee looked worried.

47

"Don't worry Wanjee, we will explain everything to you, what we do next is really fun," assured Maria. Tommy and Jake both nodded agreeing with Maria and reassuring Wanjee.

Thousands of soldier crabs and mangrove seeds assembled around the stingray hole burrowing into the sand and lining the edges to create the tunnel. Wanjee stood opened mouthed, she couldn't believe what she was witnessing. "Now comes the fun part," Maria told Wanjee.

To make sure Wanjee wasn't going to be frightened, Maria went first saying the code of silence and hovering over the stingray hole, then *WHOOSH,* she was gone.

"Where has she gone?" asked a very concerned Wanjee. "Don't worry Wanjee, we are going to a very magical place," Tommy reassured her before he, too, disappeared down the hole.

Wanjee was even more intrigued after Jake disappeared down the hole. Parlow gestured Wanjee with his wing, to go next. By now, she was quite excited and wanted to be with her friends. Tommy, Jake and Maria were waiting at the bottom, standing back excitedly waiting for Wanjee who came shooting down the hole and banged into the tunnel door. "Are you okay, Wanjee?" Maria asked, concerned.

Wanjee stood up laughing, "That was the best ride I have ever been on," she replied.

"Stand back," Maria yelled and Parlow shot down the tunnel and into the door, feathers flying everywhere.

"I thought you were going to attach pillows to the door?" Jake laughed.

"I sh-forgot," replied Parlow shaking himself off. The children all laughed and as Parlow opened the door the rainbow light shined through and onto the children.

"Warrajamba," shouted Wanjee with a big smile.

"What does that mean?" questioned Maria.

"The aboriginal people say that the rainbow serpent rose through the earth to the surface where it called all the frogs and tickled their bellies until they released water to create the pools and rivers. They call the rainbow serpent *The Mother of Life*," stated Wanjee. It is also said that when a rainbow is seen in the sky it represents the rainbow serpent moving from one water hole to another explaining why some water holes never dry up. **(5)**

The children listened in amazement and when Wanjee had completed telling the mythical story of the rainbow serpent, they all named the rainbow light 'Warrajamba'.

As they entered the Enchanted Sea World, Wanjee looked around in awe of the beauty and surprised that it was daylight. She noticed the shining golden stars against the bright blue sky and felt like she was already home. "Do you know how the stars were made?" she questioned her friends.

"No." They all replied, intrigued to hear the story.

They all stood on the golden winding path gazing up at the stars as Wanjee told the mythical story. "Aboriginal myth says there was an old man who ruled the sea, his name was Rolla-Mano. The blue ocean belonged to him, he ruled the kingdom of shadows. One day Rolla-Mano went fishing in a lonely mangrove swamp close to the shores. He caught many fish and cooked them on fire. While he was eating his fish, he noticed two beautiful women approach him with sweet voices. He grabbed his fishing net and hid in the mangrove bushes."

When the women got close enough, he threw the net over them. One of the women escaped by diving into the ocean. He jumped in after her with a fire stick in his hand, as soon as the flames hit the water, sparks scattered to the sky.

He never found the woman in the ocean and took the woman he captured up into the sky to live forever. She is the evening star glowing from her resting place. On a clear night, when you can see the sky studded with stars, they are the sparks from Rolla-Mano's fire stick, Wanjee concluded. **(6)**

Just as Wanjee had finished telling her story they heard, "Squawk, Squawk, that was an interesting story," announced Cane as he flew onto Wanjee's shoulder. "Hello, wh-my name is Cane, welcome wh-to the Enchanted Sea World," Cane said.

"Nice to meet you Cane," replied Wanjee.

"C'mon kids, we have more friends for Wanjee to meet," urged Parlow as they all began walking up the glittering golden path towards the castle.

Maria explained that they must do 1hour of school work before they can show Wanjee the rest of the Enchanted Sea World. Wanjee screwed up her nose. "Really? School work?" she said begrudgingly.

"It's okay Wanjee, you will love the way we learn here," replied Maria.

As they neared the castle Wanjee felt like she was still dreaming. The castle was laden with exotic sea shells, pearls and multi-coloured reef coral. The children introduced Wanjee to Ibis chef who was preparing a welcoming party feast for Wanjee and the children. "Ooh are you making those sherbet thingy's?" inquired Maria excitedly. Ibis never spoke much, he just gave Maria a cheeky smile.

Parlow allowed Tommy and Jake to lead the way through the red ruby door. Maria and Wanjee followed. Wanjee touched the beautiful red glistening rubies on the door as she walked into the classroom, still believing that this must all be a dream.

"Come over here and sit next to me, you can have Dino's old desk," Maria told Wanjee. As she sat at her clam shell desk chair and wondered why they were sitting near a pool. Suddenly up rose a large bald head from the water, startling Wanjee so much she fell off her chair and onto the floor. "It's okay Wanjee." Maria laughed. "This is our master teacher Wally," Maria reassured her.

Wanjee picked herself up from the floor and thought she might wake up from this strange dream soon, but it all felt so real. She sat back at her desk studying the large Dugong. "You know in our culture, you were once a real prize catch," Wanjee said to Wally.

"Oh th-dear." Wally laughed. "Well I'm th-so glad th-you have alternative th-food now," he replied with a chuckle.

"My name is Wally, nice to meet you Wanjee. I will be your master teacher for the year. It is the enchanted Sea world rule that you must complete one hour of school before you enjoy the Enchanted Sea World," he informed Wanjee, who didn't look at all impressed.

Maria noticed Wanjee's expression and went on to explain how Dino had trouble reading before Wally helped him. "Dino has dyslexia and couldn't even read when he came here but by the end of the year, with Wally's help, he was awarded Dux of the school last year," Maria encouraged Wanjee. "I guess with a Dugong as my teacher it could be fun," replied Wanjee.

The water rippled and up surfaced Pedro and Delilah from the pool, this not only startled Wanjee but she fell off her chair and seemed to be having a seizure.

The children ran over to her as she was lying on the floor shaking. "It's okay, I think she's having an 'epileptic' seizure, Grandad has had a few," said Jake who seemed to know all about it. Jake took his t-shirt off and lay it under Wanjee's head. "Don't put anything in her mouth, she will recover shortly," assured Jake. Soon enough, within 2–3 minutes Wanjee had stopped shaking and opened her eyes, rather embarrassed that she had a seizure in front of her friends.

"It's okay Wanjee, my grandad has epilepsy. Do you have any medication?" queried Jake.

"I have some special oil in this little bottle around my neck. It's from a leaf where my people come from. I didn't take any last night," she informed them as she showed the children the little bottle attached to a leather necklace around her neck.

"Okay, well, at least we know now," replied Tommy. Wanjee took the lid off her bottle and let one drop of oil under her tongue.

"I will be okay now," Wanjee assured the others and they all sat back at their desks.

Maria knew nothing about epilepsy and was concerned and wanted to know more. "What is epilepsy?" Maria asked Wanjee.

"Well, it's like too many electrical currents running through my brain at the same time," answered Wanjee.

"Is it dangerous for you?" Maria continued.

"No, I can do everything everyone else can do, I just have to make sure I take my medication," replied Wanjee.

To lighten things up a bit, Wally transferred the children's multiplication song to the virtual whiteboard. The music began and the children began singing their time tables.

Wanjee smiled and sang along, studying Delilah wearing bright pink spectacles, who she thought looked ridiculously funny, and continued singing the 2x tables trying not to laugh.

2x1=2 Buckle my shoe
2x2=4 Knock on the door
2x3=6 pick up sticks
2x4=8 shut the gate
2x5=10 big fat hen
2x6=12 dig and delve
2x7=14 words are sorting
2x8=16 flour sifting
2x9=18 play is waiting
2x10=20 games a plenty
2x11=22 cut and glue
2x12=24 as before

3x1=3 you and me
3x2=6 Pick up sticks
3x3=9 rain and shine
3x4=12 Dig and Delve
3x5= 15 time is shifting
3x6= 18 We are waiting
3x7=21 Lots of fun
3x8=24 do some more
3x9=27 My little heaven
3x10=30 Don't get dirty
3x11=33 touch your knee
3x12=36 We can fix

Wanjee was enjoying singing the times tables. Tommy, Jake and Maria knew the 2 times and 3 times tables off by heart and were keen to start the next two levels. "We will learn a th-new song for the 4x table next th-week," announced Wally.

"OH, OH, OH." The children echoed in disappointment.

"Okay th-we will do the 4x tables rh-up to 4x6," compromised Wally.

"YAY, YAY, YAY." The children yelled out together and began singing the 4x table from the whiteboard.

4x1 = 4 knock on the door
4x2=8 Close the gate
4x3=12 dig and delve
4x4=16 lean queen
4x5=20 food a plenty

"Now I would like th-you all to write a page about what th-you did in the holidays," instructed Wally.

"I'm not very good at writing," Wanjee said sadly to Wally.

"I will help th-you improve. You can tell me about what th-you did and I will transfer the th-words to the virtual whiteboard and th-you can copy the words," Wally encouraged Wanjee.

Wanjee began to tell Wally what she did over the holidays while the other three children began writing. "I made boomerangs every day," Wanjee began.

"Oh that sounds interesting, How do you make a boomerang?" inquired Wally with intrigue. Tommy, Jake and Maria stopped writing when they heard what Wanjee could do and were keen to learn how to make a boomerang. "Hey you three keep writing, Wanjee can read her story once we have finished," instructed Wally.

Wanjee continued, "First you need to find some hardwood roots, Eucalyptus roots are good but the roots must be soft. You can find soft roots by the edge of dams, lakes or rivers. There is a dam not far from where I live with Eucalyptus trees around the perimeter. I break off some soft eucalyptus roots with a sharp rock, split the root in half and shape it to look like a boomerang. Wally was transferring her words onto the whiteboard as Wanjee was telling her story. Then when the root is dry you can paint it. I painted aboriginal pictures on mine. You use a small rounded stick to make dots and you can use the red, brown and white clay found near the beaches as paint." **(7)**

"Well th-that is very clever, did th-you make boomerangs every day?" questioned Wally.

"Just about every day, I enjoy making them," replied Wanjee.

Maria put her pen down, turned to Wanjee and said, "Maybe you could show us how to make a boomerang," she said enthusiastically.

"I would be honoured to teach you," replied Wanjee and wrote her story from the whiteboard into her book.

Wally asked Maria to read her story first, then Jake, Tommy and lastly, Wanjee. The children were intrigued with Wanjee and the amazing things they were learning about her and her aboriginal culture.

"Could you teach us to make a boomerang after we show you the Enchanted Sea World?" asked Tommy.

"Please, please," Jake and Maria pleaded with her.

"Yes of course," Wanjee said happy to show her friends.

Parlow was lying on his golden throne at the entrance of the castle when the children were excused from class to enjoy the Enchanted Sea World. Jake ran outside enthusiastically, "We are going to show Wanjee the Enchanted Sea World and Wanjee is going to show us how to make a boomerang," Jake told Parlow as they passed him on the way out.

Parlow laughed. "Yes I know, go and enjoy yourselves and remember to listen for the dinner bell," replied Parlow.

The children's clamshell carts were parked in tandem beside the castle. Wanjee was excited to have her own cart. "These are amazing," she said jumping into her cart.

"They only have one speed, so no racing." Jake laughed. Tommy lead the way then Jake, Maria and Wanjee at the rear.

Maria kept turning her head back to Wanjee, pointing things out. "Over there to the left is the vegetable patch, to the right are all the fruit trees and a bit further up in the distance you will see something amazing," Maria told Wanjee.

As Wanjee was admiring the abundance of fresh fruit, Cane flew down to her cart with a large fresh mango he had sliced in half with his beak and handed it to Wanjee. She took one bite, mango juice trickled down her chin, she had never tasted a sweeter or juicier mango in all her life. "Oh these are delicious, thank you, Cane," she said. Still holding the other mango half Cane flew over to Maria's cart and handed her the mango.

"Oh thank you, Cane, you thoughtful feathery friend," said Maria.

"Hey what about us?" Called out the boys in front with a laugh. Cane squawked flew off and came back with another mango sliced in half by his beak and handed one half mango to each of the boys.

"Look ahead," called back Tommy to Wanjee. Wanjee looked over to see the Ferris wheel turning and a giant Goanna wearing sunglasses.

"You have to be kidding me," Wanjee stated in absolute disbelief.

"That's Joanna," Maria called back to Wanjee excited for her to meet their talking reptile friend and have a ride on the Ferris wheel.

The children parked their carts and introduced Joanna to Wanjee. "Goo-hello," Joanna said to Wanjee extending a long claw out for her to shake. Wanjee reluctantly used one finger to carefully shake Joanna's claw. The other children laughed.

"All the animals here are friendly, let's go for a Ferris wheel ride," said Tommy as Joanna stopped the Ferris wheel for them to climb aboard. Tommy and Jake took the first clamshell chair and Maria and Wanjee rode in the one behind the boys.

As they rotated higher, Wanjee pointed her finger towards the dolphins she could see in the distance having a play. "Mami **(8.p.74),**" she called out, her voice echoing into the gully, and the fish and dolphins all looked up. "That's the name for fish in our language," Wanjee explained.

"What do you call the whales over there?" questioned Maria.

"We call them, Kodoli **(9.p.79),**" Wanjee replied.

Maria repeated the words, "Mami, Kodoli."

"That's very martung, Maria, **(10. p.57),**" replied Wanjee.

"What does that mean?" Maria laughed.

"It means good," Wanjee replied.

"You will be speaking my language fluently soon," stated Wanjee. Both the girls laughed as they completed two rotations on the Ferris wheel.

"Time to take Wanjee to the water slide," the boys called out. Wanjee's eyes opened wide in excited anticipation of a water slide.

"Stop the Ferris wheel, please, Joanna," instructed Jake.

The children thanked Joanna, jumped into their carts and proceeded along the winding path towards the 2km water slide. As they approached the bottom of the water slide and parked their carts, Wanjee was astounded to see an enormous turtle also wearing sunglasses at the bottom of the water slide waiting for the children with a big broad smile.

"This is Mut and his brother Tut is at the top, you will meet him once we get up there on the chair lift," said Maria. The boys went first, Maria allowed Wanjee to go next she thought she might need help but it was easy for Wanjee with her long legs and she was on the chair lift without a problem.

The chair lifts climbed slowly up the hill beside the water slide, until they reached the top and jumped off. "Hello, my friends," said Tut to the children and passed them all a seaweed mat. The boys didn't hesitate, quickly taking a mat and shooting down the slide yelling out with excitement, "Weeeee, Woo-hoo," and laughing all the way to the bottom.

"You go next, Wanjee," urged Maria, passing Wanjee a seaweed mat. Down she went like a shooting star, laughing all the way to the bottom. Maria came speeding down behind her like a rocket. Both the girls rolled around at the bottom laughing so hard they were crying until their bellies ached. "Stop laughing," said Maria.

"You stop laughing," replied Wanjee and that made the girls laugh even harder.

The boys were laughing at the girls until Jake realised time was ticking and he still wanted Wanjee to show them how to make a boomerang. "Hey girls, we have enough time before our feast for Wanjee to show us how to make a boomerang," said Jake who always wanted to do as much as possible in the time they had in their happy place.

"Okay, okay," Maria said giggling, "but first let's get the puffa fish to dry us." When Maria said dried by puffa fish Wanjee started laughing loudly again.

"Pufferfish? Hahaha, dry us? Hahaha."

They began walking towards the water edge and called out, "Duff, duff, duff." Hundreds of little puffer fish popped their heads out of the water and began blowing air all over the children.

Wanjee couldn't stop laughing at what she was seeing and what the pufferfish was doing as she turned around letting the pufferfish dry her. "This is the most spectacular, amazing place in the whole world," said Wanjee who was having the best time of her life and hoped that it wasn't all a dream.

Once the children were all dry, Wanjee pointed to some eucalyptus trees not far from the water's edge. "Those trees will be perfect for our boomerangs. Close to the water, their roots will be soft. Find a sharp-edged rock first," instructed Wanjee.

The children all searched and found a sharp-edged rock then followed Wanjee who was trekking toward the eucalyptus trees. The children stood back and watched as Wanjee bent down and removed the grass on the ground a few feet away from the base of the tree. Beneath the grass was a mass of tree roots. Wanjee grabbed a root, lifted her arm holding the rock and slammed her rock down onto the root several times until it broke. She pulled the root up until she had 30cm in length and again raised her arm and slammed the rock onto the root until it snapped. "Okay your turn guys," Wanjee said as she turned around with the root piece in her hand.

Tommy, Jake and Wanjee began pulling out the grass around the roots and copied exactly what Wanjee had done. "Mine isn't breaking," announced Maria.

"Make sure you have the sharp edge of the rock facing the root," explained Wanjee. So Maria turned the rock around and slammed the root snapping it out of the ground. They all had a 30cm piece of root in their hands.

"Now bend the roots into a boomerang shape and lay the roots in the sun," instructed Wanjee. They all followed Wanjee's instructions and bent the roots into a symmetrical arch resembling a boomerang and lay the roots in the sun to dry. **(11)**

"Now, we all need to find a round-ended stick, about the size of a paintbrush," said Wanjee as she was pulling branches down to study the shapes of the twigs. The others did as Wanjee was doing. Once they had found their paintbrush sticks, Wanjee made her way over to the sandy banks of the ocean. "We need to find some clay, but we will need something to put it into," she said walking up the bank towards an acorn tree.

"These hollow nutshells will be perfect," Wanjee said as she picked three nutshells off the ground. The others did the same and followed Wanjee back to the clay. Wanjee bent down using her finger she scooped up some red mud out and into one of the shells. Mixed through the red mud were stripes of white and light brown mud. Wanjee carefully separated the white clay and put it into another nut, doing the same with the light brown clay.

The others followed what Wanjee had done and they all had their little pots of mud paint. "C'mon guys, let's see if the roots have dried," said Wanjee making her way back to the roots. The roots had dried out and ready to complete.

"How can we paint with a stick?" questioned Jake.

"It's called dot painting," replied Wanjee. "Take the rounded edge of your stick, choose a colour and dab it on the root," explained Wanjee.

The others watched as Wanjee showed them how to make an aboriginal dot painting on their boomerangs. "Wow that looks awesome, you're painting the rainbow serpent!" said Maria highly impressed. "I think I will paint the stars on mine," said Maria as she began dot painting stars on her boomerang.

"Mine is going to have a dot dolphin," announced Jake and Tommy painted a dotted turtle on his. The clay dried very quickly and the children were eager to try their boomerangs to see if they could actually fly and return to them.

"Let's go to the top of the hill and let them go from there," said Jake enthusiastically. They all climbed to the top of the hill and cast the boomerangs into the sky. Wanjee had cast hers in the direction of South Seabrooke island while the others had cast theirs over the ocean. A few seconds past and suddenly they saw their boomerangs returning back towards them. "Oh wow, they are coming back to us," screamed Jake. The children got ready to catch them as they came flying back, but Wanjee's boomerang didn't come back.

"Where is your boomerang?" questioned Maria.

"I don't know, I cast it towards South Seabrooke island," said Wanjee a little disappointed. The children sat on the grass at the top of the hill for several minutes, waiting for Wanjee's boomerang to come back. Just as they were about to leave, Wanjee saw her Boomerang coming back but it appeared to have something attached to it.

As it got nearer Wanjee stood up and held out her hand to catch it. Attached to the boomerang was a piece of bark tied on with some twine. On the bark, written in charcoal were the words, "Martu karu, we love you, Wanjee xx." Wanjee's eyes lit up, it was a note from her tribe.

"The boomerang made it all the way to South Seabrooke Island, my tribe must have recognised my painting, I always put a 'W' on my pictures," she said with excitement.

"Can I see it?" asked Maria.

Wanjee handed her the bark note. "What does Martu Karu mean?" inquired Maria.

"It means 'good day' in our language," replied Wanjee.
(12)

Wanjee knew she could now send messages to her people using her boomerang and would think about what message she would send to them next week.

"Ding, Ding, Ding," the dinner bell echoed loudly throughout the Enchanted Sea World and the children quickly started running down the hill with their boomerangs to their carts.

"Hurry, it's time to have a feast you will never forget," said Jake to Wanjee, as he ran down the hill waving his boomerang in the air.

The children got into their carts and headed straight towards the Shell Castle down the winding golden path.

Wanjee was admiring this beautiful land they called the Enchanted Sea World, she had never felt this much joy in all her life and hoped she wouldn't wake and discover it had all been a dream.

As the children approached the castle, Maria could see a sign hanging from the castle entrance. She turned around to point the sign out to Wanjee. Wanjee looked up at a sign that was written with dot letters.

"WELCOME WANJEE
TO THE ENCHANTED SEA WORLD,
OUR FAMILY IS YOUR FAMILY"

Wanjee felt very special and very loved, she parked her cart with the other children and proceeded to walk inside.

There in front of them on the dining table was a feast of food including; chocolate-coated ice cream and sherbet balls.

"Those are delicious and a mouth sensation, they will either be icy cold or give you a fizz bang experience in your mouth," Maria told Wanjee who picked one up and put it in her mouth. Suddenly, she had a mouth explosion of fizz bang and the children all began laughing.

Once they were all seated at the table, Wanjee didn't know what she would try next as there was so much food to choose from; mango and pawpaw sours, pineapple, apple and cherry fairy floss, banana bangs, strawberry all-day suckers and mini potato pies. She had never seen so much food in all her life so decided to put one of each thing on her plate. Ibis came out of the kitchen with a jug of coloured pinkish, brown liquid. The children became very excited as they recognised the four-flavour fizz bang pop drink that Ibis had made for Maria's birthday last year.

"Oh Wanjee wait until you have some of this soda drink, it's magical," said Maria.

Ibis filled the children's glasses with the four-flavour fizz-pop drink, a mixture of lemon, lime, strawberry and banana. Wanjee was thirsty and began gulping her drink down. Suddenly she did an enormous burp and a gigantic bubble came out of her mouth and landed on Maria who began floating into the air inside the bubble laughing until the bubble popped and she fell to the floor. Wanjee couldn't believe what had just happened. "Burp Maria, and blow a bubble onto me," Wanjee laughed pleading with Maria.

Maria laughed and burped at the same time and a large bubble landed on Wanjee who was now floating inside the bubble. Tommy had blown a bubble onto Jake and Maria burped another bubble onto Tommy. The children were all floating around the dining room laughing inside the bubbles until they popped and fell to the ground.

"You were right, Maria, this is the best," said Wanjee drinking some more. Parlow had left the dining room while the children were enjoying their fizz pop drink and re-entered carrying a bag.

"Hu hum," he said. "Now, you funny kids please refrain from burping for a minute, I have something to give to Wanjee." The children were keen to know what Parlow had in the bag and stopped burping bubbles. "We, your family of the Enchanted Sea World, would like you to accept this gift, it is something you need," announced Parlow.

Wanjee thanked Parlow as he handed her the bag. She opened it up and pulled out a new school uniform, a new pair of shoes, new jeans and a new pink t-shirt. "Oh thank you, Parlow, my clothes have holes in them and too small for me now, these are the perfect size," as she tried on the jeans and shoes. "How did you know what size I was?" she questioned Parlow. Parlow just smiled and before he could reply Jake answered,

"Parlow knows everything."

Wanjee went to speak again but instead let out a huge burp bubble that landed on Parlow. The children laughed as Parlow floated into the air inside the bubble but his beak soon popped the bubble and he flew to the floor. "C'mon kids, unfortunately, it is time to leave now," said Parlow with a laugh.

"Oh, I wish we could stay here forever," replied Wanjee.

"You are a part of this family forever," replied Parlow. Wanjee gave Parlow an affectionate hug and the children helped clear the table with Ibis thanking him for the delicious feast.

Then the children heard that familiar "pop, pop, pop," sound and knew who it was. "Wanjee hold your nose, Cram's food is talking." Laughed Jake.

"Oh yuck," said Wanjee holding her nose. "Who is Cram?" she questioned. Maria pointed over towards the kitchen at Cram the Crab. The children grabbed their boomerangs off the dining table and ran outside holding their noses and laughing. Wanjee hesitated, quickly grabbed some food, wrapped it in a palm leaf and stuffed it into the bag of clothes, running outside with the others.

"He does it after every meal," Maria told Wanjee. "Maybe he should eat outside." Wanjee laughed.

As they all walked down the golden winding path towards the tunnel, the children explained to Wanjee that going back up the tunnel was quite different to coming down. "The Dugongs will squirt us up," said Maria with a smile.

"Squirt us up?" questioned Wanjee in surprise.

"You will see," replied Tommy as he stood in front of the tunnel doorway.

Wanjee could see whales near the shoreline tilting their massive bodies sideways. Tommy was surprised to see whales.

"Hey where are the Dugongs?" questioned Tommy.

"Sh-it's the whale's turn this year." Parlow laughed. Then, like the force of a fireman's hose the whale squirted water from the hole in its back and in an instant Tommy shot up the hole. Jake went next and Maria offered Wanjee to go after Jake but she said she would go last thinking to herself, *if this is a dream I want to remember everything in it*, and she glanced around at the Enchanted Sea World.

After Maria had shot up the tunnel by the water, Wanjee stood waiting for her turn and saw Cane fly overhead. "Wuwu wingga," (Goodbye friend) she called out and Cane gave her a high pitched "Squwak" in return.

Wanjee waved goodbye with her bag of clothes and boomerang in one hand and stood in front of the tunnel doorway. The whale squirted another force of water that shot Wanjee straight up the tunnel landing her beside Maria on Mangrove Sands. Parlow soon followed and the soldier crabs suddenly disappeared as did the tunnel.

The children were all wet but Tommy had remembered to bring a towel which he had wrapped around his body under his t-shirt. "Here you go guys, dry off with this towel," Tommy offered. The children all dried themselves and climbed onto Parlow's back, this time Wanjee went in front of Maria so she wouldn't fall off when Parlow landed.

As Parlow ascended up into the sky towards the Northern end of the island, Maria leant over and whispered into Wanjee's ear. "Isn't it grand!" she said softly. Wanjee nodded and gave Maria a huge smile, she had never felt this happy in all her life, even if she woke up soon and discovered it was all a dream, it was the best dream she had ever had.

Parlow began descending to drop Wanjee home first as her house was the closest to Mangrove Sands. Maria whispered again into Wanjee's ear, "Make sure you hide your ingot in a secret and safe spot when you get home."

"I will," replied Wanjee.

"And you cannot say a word about this to anyone or your ingot will dissolve," continued Maria.

"I promise, who would believe me anyway," she said with a laugh.

Parlow landed on Wanjee's window sill, all was quiet on the home front. Wanjee climbed off Parlow's back and thanked him for the clothes and the wonderful time she had. "You are sh-welcome. Hold your ingot and sh-say the code of silence," Parlow instructed. Wanjee did as she had been asked and began floating back into her body which lay in her bed.

"Wuwu Wingga," she said lying in her bed.

"Wuwu Wingga," they all replied to Wanjee as Parlow flew off the window sill into the sky.

After they had gone, Wanjee took off her ingot from around her neck and placed it at the back of the picture frame she had of her parents. She proceeded to carefully fold her new clothes and hung her new school dress up for school on Monday. A small shoebox lay in the corner inside her cupboard, Wanjee carefully put the food she had grabbed from her feast, into the box for the next day.

As she lay her boomerang next to the photo of her parents, there were no tears, when she said good night to the picture of her parents, instead, she said, "You will be happy to know I am being well looked after by a new family in a secret place called the Enchanted Sea World. I know I will see you again one day. Goodnight, I love you both." She climbed into bed, feeling the happiest she had ever felt and continued to hope that tonight had not just been a dream.

(5) Maddock, Kenneth (1978) **The rainbow serpent Dream time story** https://en.m.wikipedia.org/wiki/Rainbow-Serpent

Warrajamba

(6) (7) Muruppi.com www.sacred-texts.com

(8 p.74)(9 p.79)(10 p.57) Muandik/Bunganditj Language Reclamation Project, November 2012. Burrandies Aboriginal Corporation, 49 Helen Street (PO Box 2500) Mt Gambier SA 5290.

(11) Muruppi.com www.sacred-texts.com

(12 p.45) Muandik/Bunganditj Language Reclamation Project, November 2012. Burrandies Aboriginal Corporation, 49 Helen Street (PO Box 2500) Mt Gambier SA 5290.

Chapter 4

Burning Embers

It was 7.30 am the following morning when Wanjee awoke to the sounds of arguing but for some reason it did not bother her today, she was feeling happy remembering a wonderful magical dream. *Or was it a dream?* She looked over to the small dressing table and saw a boomerang next to the photo frame. She quickly turned the photo over and sure enough, on the back was a golden ingot with the code of silence inscribed around the perimeter. She could hardly contain her overwhelming joy and began dancing around her room hardly noticing her foster parents arguing in the next room. She opened her cupboard and there were her new clothes and a small box of delicious treats. Quickly, putting on her new jeans and bright pink t-shirt she laced up her new shoes, grabbed the box of delicious enchanted treats and tiptoed past her foster parents' bedroom and outside to her bright pink bike.

Down the dirt road and onto the main concrete footpath, she peddled as fast as her long legs would take her, towards Maria's house. She was bursting to talk with Maria about the Enchanted Sea World and their adventures last night.

By the time Wanjee arrived at Maria's house, she was panting with beads of sweat pouring down her face. She came tearing into Maria's driveway, skidding the bike sideways to a halt and running to the front door, knocking loudly. "Hold on, hold on, I'm coming," shouted Maria.

When the door opened, Wanjee wrapped her arms around Maria and said, "It wasn't a dream, it was real," Wanjee blurted out, breathless.

Maria laughed and said quietly, "Yes it was real, Wanjee, come into my bedroom and we can chat for a while but I think it's best if we get the boys and go to the 'Pina Wali'."

"Yes," giggled Wanjee, "the 'Pina Wali' is the place to talk about our secrets, of course," replied Wanjee all too excited and breathless.

"What's in the shoebox?" inquired Maria.

"Oh, I grabbed some food off the table last night when you all ran outside, we can have the treats in the 'Pina Wali'," replied Wanjee.

"Martu," (good) replied Maria.

"Wow, you sure are picking up my lingo," replied Wanjee, happy that her friends wanted to learn more of her Muandik language.

As Maria began dressing, she questioned Wanjee about her ingot. "Did you hide your ingot in a safe place?"

"Any place in my room would be safe, my foster parents never come in, I think I am quite invisible in their lives. I hid it on the back of a photo frame of my parents," she replied.

"That's good. Jake's grandfather threw his old shoes in the bin when he was away on holidays and that's where he had put his ingot."

"No! How did you find it?" Wanjee questioned Maria surprised.

"It's a long story but Shian the whistling kite and his flock of kite friends took us to Junkyard Well, flying on swings attached to the kite's feet. Ollie the octopus and his babies, who you haven't met, found it in the well last week."

"Wow, I can't wait to meet all the enchanted sea world creatures. Flying on swings? Maybe the kites can fly me to South Seabrooke Island to see my tribe?" questioned Wanjee.

"Who knows what adventures lie ahead," replied Maria putting on her favourite pale blue T-shirt and lacing her shoes up. "There, I'm ready, let's go and get Tommy and Jake," said Maria.

"Here, have a sherbet ball," said Wanjee handing Maria a sherbet ball as they climbed on their bikes.

The girls started peddling towards Jake's house, both laughing when their mouths exploded with a fizz bang of delicious sherbet. Jake was outside when the girls arrived. "Off to the 'Pina Wali'?" he called out to the girls who nodded yes as they enjoyed the last remnants of sherbet dissolving on their inner cheeks and tongue.

Jake grabbed his bike and they all began riding to Tommy's when Jake thought he smelt something that hinted at danger.

"Hey," he called back to the girls still peddling their bikes, "Do you smell smoke?" he questioned. Both the girls began sniffing like dogs on a scent, noses pointed in the air, but all they could smell was the delicious flavour of sherbet. "I can only smell my sherbet," Wanjee said laughing.

"Mmm, I think I smell some smoke but it's probably someone burning off," replied Maria not too concerned.

Maria called back to Jake, "I think someone is burning off." And the children continued towards Tommy's house. Tommy was already up and dressed and watering the garden for his grandfather when Jake, Wanjee and Maria rode into his driveway. "Hey guys, I'll grab my bike," said Tommy winding the hose up and keen to go for a ride. "Did you smell any smoke on the way over here?" Tommy asked his friends.

"Yeah but we think it's just someone burning off," replied Jake.

"C'mon guys, Wanjee has some enchanted treats from last night for our morning tea, or breakfast, if you haven't had any." She laughed.

Jake jumped on his bike, turned his head and with a cheeky smile said to Wanjee, "Race ya to the Pina Wali."

Wanjee laughed. "He will never beat me. Here, take the box of treats," she said handing the box to Maria, and off she sped standing up with her long legs pushing the peddles as fast as the speed of lightning. Jake had disappeared taking the shortcut through the bushes but Wanjee knew a quicker way and suddenly neither of them could be seen. Tommy and Maria enjoyed a casual bike ride on the footpath and laughed at Wanjee and Jake, competing like they were in the Olympics vying for the gold medal.

Maria had already taken her ingot and put it around her neck, she quickly said the code of silence and was on Parlow's back in no time. Parlow flew quickly towards Jake's house. As he began to ascend, Jake saw them and yelled, "I can't leave Grandad, he is drunk." Parlow landed in Jake's backyard and instructed the children to slump Granddad over his back and climb on. Jake had his ingot around his neck and quickly said the code of silence and the children floated Grandad onto Parlow's back.

Grandad lay in between Tommy and Jake with his large beer belly lying on Parlow's feathery back, legs dangling on one side, his arms on the other side. Parlow could feel the extra weight but managed to become airborne. As they flew towards Wanjee's home, Grandad giggled and dribbled. "Woo-hoo," he yelled out laughing, "this is the best Bourbon in town."

"Oh be quiet," Jake replied in disgust. "Don't get too close to the flames," Jake instructed Parlow. "Grandad has so much alcohol in his body, we will all go up in flames from the fumes," Jake said quite indignantly.

As Parlow descended towards Wanjee's home, they could see her standing outside with her pink bike and ingot around her neck. When Wanjee saw the heavy load Parlow was carrying, she yelled out, "Keep going Parlow, I will ride my bike."

"It's okay Parlow, Wanjee is the fastest bike rider I have ever known," Jake assured Parlow.

"Okay," replied Parlow. "Sh-See you down there," as he turned his body due South.

When Parlow arrived at Mangrove Sands, many islanders had arrived and ferries were taking them to safety on the mainland. The fire was rapidly tearing through the dense shrub. Eucalyptus trees were combusting and exploding like fireworks, continuing to spread the fires. Even the firemen were abandoning the fires and moving towards Mangrove Sands in an attempt to keep everyone safe.

The mass of evacuating Islanders was clambering onto the ferries but there were too many people for the ferries to carry and insufficient ferries. People were held back and told to wait for the next ferry or barge. The barges were slow taking one hour from the mainland and most were being used to transport the fire engines and volunteers.

Parlow landed on the sand in a secluded spot under some thick mangroves, 50 metres from the islanders who were queued up for the ferries. Jake pushed grandpa headfirst off Parlow's back landing him on his head upside down giggling and unaware of the danger approaching. "Hahahahahah." Grandpa laughed. "That was the best ride I have ever had, felt like I was flying, hahahaha," he continued laughing.

"Oh be quiet, Grandpa," Jake said frustrated, "there's a fire out of control."

"Oh," replied Grandpa, starting to come to his senses.

Wanjee arrived on her pink bike just as Parlow instructed the children to look after the islanders waiting for ferries. "Tell them sh-more help is on the sh-way."

"Okay," the children replied.

"Be quick," Tommy urged Parlow.

Parlow flew off over the smokey horizon, then he was gone, leaving the children to wonder what kind of help would be returning.

They did as Parlow had instructed them to do and began assuring, at least 2000 islanders, that more help was on its way and to stay calm.

Twenty minutes had passed since Parlow left and the children were beginning to get worried. More islanders were arriving, the smoke was increasingly thicker and bright orange flames could be seen travelling along the shoreline towards Mangrove Sands.

Then, over in the distant ocean, Tommy noticed a mass of fins travelling at speed and a school of massive humpback whales a few hundred metres hovering in the deeper waters. The calm waters rapidly turned to large rolling waves. "Stand back," shouted Tommy. "Our help has arrived." And to the islanders' surprise thousands of singing dolphins arrived in the shallow waters.

"Quick," said Tommy, "two people to every dolphin." The children assisted everyone onto the dolphins. "Hang on around the dolphin's neck and those people at the back hold onto the fin," instructed Tommy.

The dolphins floated gently into the shallow waters until all the islanders were safely accounted for and on a dolphin, all except Maria, Wanjee, Tommy, Jake, oh and Grandpa, who was slouched and snoring up against a mangrove tree.

The children stood on the shoreline watching the dolphins who gave out a high pitch squeal and carefully swimming towards the whales in the deeper water. Once the dolphins reached the majestic whales, they turned their bodies adjacent to the whales front flipper. One at a time, each dolphin dropped the islanders to the whales.

Each person climbed onto the whale's slippery ribbed flipper and up onto the whales back using the barnacles attached to the whales as steps. The largest whale at the front of the school appeared to be white, he was magnificent. Suddenly, he let out an echoing sound almost as if he was talking, almost as if he said, Bigaloo.

Then he blew water, four metres high, out of the blowhole from his back and the humpback whales gracefully began gliding on the surface of the water in convoy with each of the eleven whales carrying 200 people on their backs. All except one whale who stayed behind hovering in the deep ocean.

It was suddenly very quiet except for the penetrating snoring from grandpa. Tommy was looking over to the horizon when he saw Parlow flying towards them and pointed. "Here comes Parlow," Tommy shouted with relief and all the children cheered.

Parlow landed and with some concern in his voice told the children to climb on his back. "Jump on kids, I'll sh-get you to the mainland."

"But what about grandpa?" Jake queered as he looked at his Grandpa perched up against a mangrove tree snoring.

"We will never be able to fit five of us on your back all that way, and Grandpa isn't light," said Jake.

Parlow laughed. "I know sh-son, I know," he replied.

As Grandpa slipped from his perch on the mangrove tree and went face down into the sand a dozen fire engines began arriving in convoy. At least one hundred firemen with charcoaled faces and sweat pouring off them, slowly climbed off the trucks. They were fatigued and moved towards the beach looking defeated.

One fireman saw grandpa lying face down in the sand and went over to him. "That's my Grandpa, we don't have enough room on our friendly pelican for him," yelled Jake. "Don't worry son, we will get him to the mainland," said the fireman, who really didn't know how, as the ferries and barges had been detained now everyone was off the island.

Just as the fireman was telling Jake they would take his Grandpa a 4 metre fountain of water squirted straight up into the air and a majestic sound echoed Mangrove Sands, it was the whale who had stayed behind. The fireman stood open-mouthed in astonishment. Tommy turned to the fireman and reassured him that he was friendly. "It's okay all the sea creatures are friendly once you get to know them," said Jake to the fireman.

Again, the whale let out a massive majestic singing sound, urging the firemen to swim out to him. The dolphins returned to the shallow waters squealing for the firemen to climb on their backs. The fireman saw the flames nearing the beach and knew they had no more time to waste.

"You kids go with your friendly pelican, we will make sure grandpa makes it to the mainland safely," he assured Jake.

The children jumped on Parlow's back and flew due North over Reband Bay towards the mainland ferry terminal. As Parlow ascended into the sky Maria pointed to a sandy alcove, enclosed by a massive old timber fence, surrounded by water. "Look down there," she called out. Within the confined area was Miss Ellie, with her two Labradors 'Hoover' and 'Stoner' and all the island dogs, cats and birds.

Everyone knew Miss Ellie, she had worked at the island Primary school for a decade and arranged to stay behind to keep everyone's pets safe from the fires. She could not leave her two Labradors who were old and could not walk very far.

Suddenly Tommy witnessed an amazing sight, "Look to the west," yelled Tommy. The children saw several majestic humpback whales gliding gently through the water with their backs tilted towards the island squirting water from their blowholes and extinguishing the fires. Excitedly, Maria yelled down to miss Ellie who could not see the whales, "The fires are out, Miss Ellie."

"Shaboom, Shabang," yelled back Miss Ellie with a big smile.

The children all looked surprised. "Miss Ellie knows the code of silence," cried out Maria.

"Oh yes," replied Parlow. "I've been visiting Miss Ellie since she was your age."

Meanwhile back at Mangrove Sands, two firemen had gone over to grandpa slouched against the mangrove tree, one on either side, grabbed his arms and put them around their necks. "Oh, mate, how much have you been drinking?" questioned one of the firemen screwing up his nose. "Hahahah, enough to know I've been flying," Grandpa slurred, laughing.

All the firemen, except four, climbed onto a dolphin and were taken out to the whale. The Four firemen who stayed behind decided that grandpa would never stay on a dolphin and they would have to swim him out to the Whale.

One of the firemen grabbed a thickly braided nylon rope from the fire engine. Two firemen stood on either side of grandpa and lifted his arms around their necks. The other two firemen grabbed his legs and placed them on their shoulders. With grandpa now elevated in the air, the firemen began swimming out to the whale. Grandpa woke momentarily and laughed. "First I was flying, now I am floating above the water, hahahahah."

By the time the firemen carrying grandpa reached the whale, they were exhausted; two firemen already on the whale climbed down to the whale's flipper and lifted grandpa onto the whale then assisted their colleagues out of the water. Grandpa was too drunk to climb barnacles so the firemen tied Grandpa firmly on his back to the whale's front flipper. With one hundred firemen on his back and grandpa tied to his flipper, the whale let out a majestic singing sound, flapped its tail and gently glided through the murky brown water and thick smokey air towards the mainland.

As Parlow was descending towards the jetty on the mainland, the children could see thousands of islanders anxiously awaiting news on the fires. Parlow landed discreetly in some bushland at the rear of the jetty. "Go and inform the islanders that the firemen extinguished all the fires," Parlow told the children who looked puzzled as they knew the whales had saved the island. "We don't want to give away all our secrets, do we?" said Parlow. The children agreed and besides, the firemen had worked so hard, they deserved some recognition.

The children thanked Parlow and waved goodbye as they began informing the islanders that the firemen had extinguished the fires and the island had been saved.

Roars of excited screams and applauding could be heard for miles and then the screams suddenly stopped. What a sight to behold, one hundred firemen sitting on the back of a gigantic humpback whale with Grandpa tied to the whales front flipper.

The firemen waved their charcoaled yellow helmets at the islanders. Huge roars of "Hooray, Hooray" and applauding came from the jetty. A passenger ferry made its way out to the whale hovering in the deep water. One at a time, the firemen stepped over grandpa and climbed onto the ferry, the last two remaining untied Grandpa, dragging him up onto the ferry.

"It's about time someone untied me," Grandpa said indignantly. By this time Grandpa had sobered up somewhat and began telling the firemen on the ferry, he had a fantastic dream. "I flew in the air, floated on top of the water and rode a whale," he told them.

The firemen all began laughing, "Well the last bit is true, we did ride a whale and that is amazing, but flying?" They all began laughing again.

"Yeah, flying high on Bourbon," another fireman called out laughing.

Roars and shouts of congratulations and thanks came from the jetty as the firemen stepped off the ferry and onto the jetty. The firemen were surprised to learn that the fires were out and thought the helicopters must have finally extinguished the fires.

Jake had made his way to the ferry to see if his grandpa was okay when a very large fireman with a badge that read 'CHIEF' stopped him. "Hey son, is that your grandpa in the ferry?"

"Yeah," replied Jake a little embarrassed. "And were you with the other three children who helped everyone off the island and stayed behind?" asked the Chief.

"Yes," replied Jake.

"Well young man, the four of you are being nominated for bravery awards for what you did," said the Chief.

"Really?" replied Jake suddenly feeling quite proud of what he and his friends had done, then he remembered Miss Ellie and what she had done. "What about Miss Ellie?" Jake responded. "She saved all the islanders animals and is still on the island," Jake insisted.

"Don't worry son, we won't forget Miss Ellie," the Chief assured Jake.

Once the island was deemed safe to return, the ferries started their engines ready to take the islanders home. As everyone queued up to start boarding, a loud majestic sound came from the ocean, water squirted four metres high and the whale breached and plunged into the ocean, swimming out to sea.

When the islanders arrived back to Mangrove Sands, although all the homes had been saved, most of the dense scrub had been destroyed and nothing but burning embers and smouldering trees remained. The islanders were just thankful that their homes, animals and everyone had survived.

It had been a very long and exhausting day. The children said goodbye at the ferry, as everyone walked home with their families. Jake's Grandpa kept repeating his exciting adventure.

"I was flying hahaha, floating hahaha," Grandpa kept repeating himself as he staggered home.

"Just lay off the bourbon Grandpa, you could have been killed," said a frustrated Jake.

Chapter 5

Enemy Feud

It was Monday morning, the day after the fires and although the island bushland was still smouldering, the day continued as normal. Wanjee got up extra early and walked to Mangrove Sands to collect her bike that she had left there during the fires. The children met on their bikes as usual commenting on the burning embers and how clever the sea creatures were by extinguishing the fires and saving everyone. They hurried into school and lined up for the school assembly.

Every Monday morning was school assembly where students received certificates and awards for excellence and for achieving their goals.

This particular assembly was different. There were far more parents and islanders in the assembly area today, even the local newspaper reporter was there. The students were beginning to line up and sit down in the large, outdoor undercover area. Jake had just taken his seat and noticed six well-dressed firemen arriving outside the school in their bright red fire truck. "Oh no, not another fire," he said under his breath, but to Jake's relief, the firemen came up onto the stage and sat on chairs provided for them. The largest of the firemen, holding a box, looked familiar to Jake, it was the fireman who spoke to him at the ferry yesterday.

Once all the students were seated, the principal stood at the podium and spoke about how lucky everyone was to have been saved by such heroic firemen, the audience applauded and the principal asked the Chief to come forward.

The Chief was a tall, solid man who held his chest out and shoulders back, he had a commanding presence and when he spoke his voice was deep and penetrating, everyone listened.

"Good morning all," he began. "You may believe that the firemen and volunteers are the heroes that saved your island yesterday but let me tell you, the true heroes of yesterday's island inferno were four students and one former teacher at your school. Not only did these students and this teacher help the islanders and animals stay safe and evacuate, they all stayed behind until every islander was safely off the island, all except Miss Ellie who remained on the island looking after the animals."

The students, parents and visitors began applauding and cheering very loudly. The Chief raised his large hand and immediately everyone was silent. "The local fire brigade wishes to acknowledge these heroic people with a bravery award. Please come forward, Tommy, Jake, Maria, Wanjee and Miss Ellie." The children felt extremely proud as the large

Chief handed each of them a gold medallion that read, "Bravery award for a heroic act."

More cheers and applauding erupted from the assembly. Tommy thanked the Chief and stood up to the podium. "Thank you sir, we are honoured but we believe the true heroes are the dolphins and humpback whales." Everyone applauded yet again acknowledging the majestic, heroic sea creatures. The reporter took several photos of the children and Miss Ellie with their bravery awards before the students were instructed to go to class. Wanjee held her bravery award with pride.

"This is the first award I have ever received," she told Jake.

"Well, you couldn't get one better than this," he replied with a proud broad smile.

As the days passed, the smoke and embers peated out and by the end of the week green regrowth and vegetation had already begun sprouting up from the soil.

The week passed quickly and the children were excited to go to the enchanted sea world. Wanjee planned on sending a message on her boomerang to her tribe on South Seabrooke Island and was eager to meet Ollie, the babies and Shian.

After the children rode home they completed their chores quickly, as they always did every Friday evening and prepared for their Enchanted Sea World adventure. Tommy made sure he had a towel and his ingot, Jake climbed under his bed and took his ingot out from the shoe box, Maria always put her ingot on before she climbed into bed and Wanjee stuffed a spare empty cotton bag down her jeans so she could bring home some food again. She grabbed her boomerang then went outside and found a piece of bark and a charcoaled stick she put in her pocket.

Parlow arrived on Tommy's window sill right on time at 7 pm and in turn collected Jake, Maria and Wanjee. When they arrived at Mangrove Sands, Parlow congratulated the children for their efforts during the fires. "Well done to all of you last week, I would say it was a very good team effort!" he told them.

The children agreed and wondered if Dino had heard about the fires. "Does Dino know about the fires last week?" Jake asked Parlow.

"I would say so, you all had your heroic faces planted all sh-over the local sh-newspaper this week," replied Parlow with a smile. The children laughed, said the code of silence and shot down the tunnel the soldier crabs had made for them. This time when they landed they were cushioned by a pillow attached to the tunnel door.

"That was a softer landing," announced Tommy.

"Thank goodness Parlow remembered the cushion this week," stated a grateful Maria. The children all stood back allowing Parlow to gently land into the pillow. "Ah, sh-that was a better landing," he announced with a smile. The children thanked Parlow for remembering the pillow. The tunnel door opened and in shone the rainbow light.

"Warrajamba, the rainbow serpent," the children all said at once.

"Yes," Parlow replied, "the mother of life," and gave Wanjee a smile and a wink as they all began to walk up the winding golden path towards the shell castle.

"Squawk, Squawk," a noisy Cane flew over the children excited to see them once again. "Hi Wingga (hello friend)," Wanjee called out laughing. Cane flew straight down to Wanjee and sat on her shoulder until they reached the castle.

Tommy, Jake and Maria also said hello to Cane using Wanjee's language. "Hi Wingga Cane." They all repeated.

"Wh-hi Wingga," replied Cane.

The children began laughing.

"Now Cane is talking my language." Wanjee laughed quite proudly.

When the children entered the castle, Ibis was running around with fresh vegetables in his tall white chef's hat and long skinny legs. He became very excited when he was preparing food. He waved a feathered wing at the children and continued running in and out of the kitchen. The children continued along the corridor and through the red ruby door. Cane was still sitting on Wanjee's shoulder when the children all sat at their clam seats at their desks when Wally poked his huge bald head out of the pool, then Delilah and Pedro.

"Good th-evening children," Wally said in a deep slow sounding tone.

"Good evening Wally," the children replied.

"I believe th-you are to be commended on your heroic acts of bravery th-this week," said Wally.

"Well, it was really the dolphins and whales who deserve all the credit," replied Tommy.

"You also did th-your part and we are all very proud of th-you," said Wally with Delilah, Pedro and Cane all nodding their heads in approval.

Then Wally transferred the times tables song to the virtual whiteboard and the children began singing.

3x1=3 you and me
3x2=6 Pick up sticks
3x3=9 rain and shine

3x4=12 Dig and Delve
3x5= 15 time is shifting
3x6= 18 We are waiting
3x7=21 Lots of fun
3x8=24 do some more
3x9=27 My little heaven
3x10=30 Don't get dirty
3x11=33 touch your knee
3x12=36 We can fix

"And th-now the 4 times table to 12," Instructed Wally with a smile.

4x2=8 Close the gate
4x3=12 dig and delve
4x4=16 lean queen
4x5=20 food a plenty
4x6=24 Red Ruby door
4x7=28 This is great
4x8=32 This is new
4x9=36 We can fix
4x10=40 We're not naughty
4x11=44 We want more
4x12=48 never too late

The children repeated their times tables songs several times, clapping and laughing as they sang, suddenly Wally turned the virtual whiteboard off "Ah," the children echoed in disappointment.

"You all have free time now to write or create anything you wish," instructed Wally.

"Oh wow, I might draw an aboriginal dot drawing of the mythical story about Rolla_Mano," said Maria all excited.

Tommy decided to write a letter to Dino and draw a picture of the dolphins and whales rescuing the islanders. Jake also decided to write a note to Dino and draw the firemen taking grandpa across the water to the humpback whale.

Wanjee was going to use this time to write a note to her tribe. She took the charcoaled stick and piece of bark out of her back pocket and began writing in charcoal on the bark.

'Yuru'(hello), I hope this letter finds you. How are my parents? Please
send them my love. Tell them, 'Ngathu martung' (13.
p.31)(I'm well), I have new friends
and I hope to see you all soon.
'Wuwu wingga', (Goodbye friend).
Love W x.

Wanjee could only write a small note as she couldn't fit any more writing on her piece of bark. The school hour was over and the children were free to go and have fun in the Enchanted Sea World. "May I take this note with me?" Wanjee asked Wally.

"Let me th-have a look at it first please," replied Wally in his deep voice. Wanjee handed her piece of bark to Wally who read the note. "This is th-a very nice message, I like the way th-you used some of your language. How th-are you posting it?" questioned Wally.

"Via this boomerang," replied Wanjee with a smile holding her boomerang.

"Very clever," replied Wally.

The children tidied their desks, thanked their tutors and raced outside. "First we must introduce Wanjee to Shian and Ollie," stated Tommy getting into his cart.

"I must send my note," replied Wanjee.

"No problem, we can do that from the top of the hill that overlooks Ollie's cave," replied Jake.

The children drove their carts past Joanna at the Ferris wheel giving him a wave. They waved as they drove past Mut and Tut at the water slide and began climbing the steep water slide hill in their carts.

Once they had reached the top of the hill, the children parked their carts next to the oak trees. Tommy started calling out "Kerwark, kerwark," suddenly Shian swooped past the children and landed on a eucalyptus branch above them.

"Hey Shian, we want you to meet Wanjee," Tommy said with Shian looking intently at him with his glowing yellow eyes.

"Kerwark, kerwark, hallo," replied Shian.

"You are beautiful," replied Wanjee, who was in awe of Shian's large graceful wings and glowing yellow eyes. "Please excuse me," said Wanjee to Shian, "but I must cast this boomerang towards South Seabrooke island, it is a message for my tribal family," explained Wanjee to Shian.

Wanjee had attached the bark with a piece of vine, tucked the boomerang into her chest and cast it towards South Seabrooke Island.

Shian let out a "Kerwark, kerwark" and followed the boomerang into the distance.

"It could be some time before the boomerang returns, we might have time to meet Ollie," said Wanjee with excitement.

"We must walk carefully down this rock face towards that cave below," instructed Tommy to Wanjee. Tommy noticed that Ollie and the babies were not standing at the mouth of the cave which they usually did when they saw or heard the children on a Friday night. The children carefully climbed over the rugged hill face until they were standing in front of Ollie's cave. Still, there was no sign of Ollie or the babies.

"Well, that is very odd," stated Tommy as the others stood at the mouth of the cave looking quite puzzled.

"Where is everyone?" Maria exclaimed.

"I have no idea, but we will find out," replied Tommy leading everyone into the cave. The children began calling out, "Ollie? Harry? Larry? Mow? Pippa?" The children's voices echoed throughout the cave but still there was no reply.

Tommy led the way through the cave until they reached the rock pool full of exotic fish and multi-coloured corals. Wanjee was so amazed at the beauty beneath the water and wanted to stop and observe the fish and corals. "These are the most beautiful corals, look at all the colours, vivid aqua, tangerine, ruby red, oh and look at the fish, they are the same colour. Look, they're camouflaging themselves in the coral," Wanjee exclaimed with joy.

"Sorry Wanjee, you can look at the pool another day, we must keep moving, I feel something is terribly wrong with our friends," replied a concerned Tommy.

The children kept moving and hit the end of the tunnel leading them to South Seabrooke Island. "Hey, this island is where I am from, but we are on the Northern end, along the way from here," said a surprised Wanjee. "I don't need to use the kites swing to see my people after all," said a joyous Wanjee.

"We must keep moving," said Tommy who could neither see nor hear his friends. Just as the children came to the Southern tip of the island, they saw Ollie in the ocean looking extremely distressed. "Hey Ollie, what's wrong?" Tommy called out to Ollie who was in the water searching for something.

"My ph-babies are gone, gone," he said whimpering. "I let them ph-go adventuring this morning and they didn't come back," Ollie said sadly swimming over to the children.

"Hello, ph-you must be Wanjee," Ollie said.

"Hello Ollie, yes I am and I'm sorry about your babies," said Wanjee sympathetically.

"I have searched ph-for hours and there is no sign of them," said Ollie sadly as he began swimming back towards the cave in the shallow water as the children followed him along the shore. Just as they had reached the entrance to the cave, they heard four squeaky voices spluttering and swimming as fast as a torpedo behind them.

"Help papa, help papa, he took us but we escaped, he ph-is coming after ph-you papa," said Harry, Larry, Mow and Pip, wrapping their tentacles around Ollie.

"Oh my babies, you ph-are back, I thought I had lost ph-you forever," said a relieved Ollie. "Ph-who is coming after me?" questioned Ollie.

"He said he ph-is our father, ph-his name is Archie and ph-he is a really huge octopus papa," said Larry with fear.

"Oh no," said Tommy. "When we caught your babies in the pipe last year, we didn't think about who they belonged to, we just wanted you to have a family," said Tommy realising what had happened.

"But I have raised them, they ph-are my family," said Ollie firmly.

"OMG! Look out behind you, Ollie," gasped Jake as an enormous octopus came flying out of the water and onto Ollie's head. The two octopus wrestled each other, tentacles and arms wrapping, flapping and splashing around each other, spitting blue ink until the two octopus had tied themselves together in a tangled knot, their tentacle arms entwined like liquorice sticks, they looked like blue tie-died wet rags.

The babies and the children began laughing at the funny sight of two octopus tied together. "Well that's a ph-fine mess you've got yourselves ph-into." Mow laughed.

The two giant octopus had tied themselves so tightly together that they were face to face and suddenly realised how silly they both looked and this was not going to solve the problem. "I ph-found your babies stranded and ph-have looked after them since they were very tiny," Ollie informed his enemy.

"Ph-we could settle this ph-feud if we both want what's best ph-for the babies," Archie calmed down and listened with intrigue. He was beginning to understand that if not for Ollie's care, his babies may never have survived.

"We live in this ph-very ph-very large majestic cave. Ph-you could come and live with us," suggested Ollie, remembering how sad he was before the babies arrived.

Slowly, they began to relax loosening their knotted tentacles. Archie's eyes filled with tears. "I ph-lost my partner, ph-she died in the ph-oil spill last year and I can see you have ph-looked after the babies well and they are ph-happy," replied Archie. "I think that could ph-work," said a grateful

Archie, freeing his tentacles from Ollie. The children all applauded and shouted joyfully, "YAY, YAY, YAY."

The two Octopus shook tentacle arms and began laughing at the sight of each other's blue tie-dyed looking bodies.

Once the octopus were free from each other and had made a truce, Tommy quietly whispered in Ollie's ear, "pssst, don't ever tell Archie we captured his babies for you," said a concerned Tommy.

"Not a chance son, not a chance," said Ollie giving Tommy a wink.

As they all walked into the cave, Harry, Larry, Mow and Pip extended their tentacle arms out to Wanjee introducing themselves. "Hello, slimy little creatures," Wanjee replied laughing and wiping the slime off her hands.

As they approached the rock pool, Archie was clearly impressed with his new home. "Welcome to your new ph-pad," Ollie said.

"Not bad," replied Archie who already looked like he belonged in his new home with Ollie and the babies.

The sound of a bell echoed through the cave. "We must hurry that is the meal bell," announced Tommy.

"What about my boomerang?" questioned Wanjee who suddenly remembered they had left before the boomerang had returned.

"We will look for it when we get back to our carts," assured Tommy. The children said goodbye to their friends including Archie and began trekking up the rocky hillside towards their karts.

Once they reached the top of the hill, Wanjee began looking for the boomerang. "I can't see it anywhere," she said with disappointment.

"We can't spend too much time looking, we must get back for our meal," replied Jake as they all searched for Wanjee's boomerang.

"Oh well, perhaps my tribe didn't see it when I threw it over," said a disappointed Wanjee. "We better get going," she said sadly climbing into her cart.

As the children neared the castle they heard a familiar sound. "Kerwark, kerwark." The children looked into the sky directly above them.

"It's Shian, look, he has my boomerang in his mouth," yelled out an excited Wanjee. Shian dropped the boomerang from his beak as Wanjee held her hand out of her cart catching it with precision. She stopped her cart and a new piece of bark and writing was attached to the boomerang. Wanjee read the note out loud;

"Hello, Wanjee,
We are all well. Your parents are getting better and send
their love. We are happy you have some new friends.
'Mimira-nga' (I'm glad) (14.p.31.)
We will stay in touch.
'Wuwu Wingga' (goodbye friend)
From
Your Muandik Tribe."

"Did you hear? My parents are getting better," Wanjee said with joy and a smile from ear to ear.

"That is such good news," replied Maria. Wanjee couldn't have been happier. Hearing the news that her parents were getting better gave her hope of returning to her home one day.

The children entered the castle and into the dining area met by Parlow and Cram who was sitting in the corner near the kitchen. The children were hungry and Ibis chef had prepared yet another delicious meal of fresh fruit salad, mini potato pies and delicious strawberry and banana smoothies.

"Sh-how was your adventure today?" Parlow asked the children as they sat eating their potato pies.

"You already know what we did," replied Jake laughing.

"Yes, but I like sh-hearing about what sh-you learned," replied Parlow with a smile.

"First, we learned never to take anything that doesn't belong to us unless you ask first." Tommy laughed, referring to the baby octopus. Maria put her hand up as she swallowed her last mouthful of potato pie.

"And we learned that fighting does not resolve anything, but through communicating and talking anything can be resolved," stated Wanjee.

"Very good," replied Parlow. Wanjee put her hand up. "Yes Wanjee," said Parlow.

"We learned that being disappointed doesn't mean we give up," said Wanjee with a smile.

"Remember these sh-lessons children, they will serve sh-you well throughout your entire life," replied Parlow. The children had just finished their delicious meal when a ghastly familiar odour began drifting over the dining table.

"Oh YUCK Cram, you are disgusting," cried out Jake holding his nose and jumping up from the table.

"Thank you Ibis Chef but we have to go," the children all yelled out to Ibis holding their noses, as they jumped up from the table and ran outside laughing. Wanjee pulled her bag out, grabbed a handful of everything and threw it in her bag, grabbed her boomerang and ran outside with the others.

"I think I will ban sh-you from eating inside from now sh-on," Parlow told Cram as he followed the children outside.

After the children had recovered from the stench of Cram, they began walking down the golden glittery path with Parlow who informed them that Cram would no longer be eating with them. The children all cheered and clapped their hands. "Good, no more contaminated air." Jake laughed.

The children lined up in tandem as the whales prepared to shoot water out of their blowhole. Tommy was shot up onto Mangrove Sands first, then came Maria, Jake and Wanjee. Tommy took his towel out from around his waist hidden under his T-shirt and they all quickly dried themselves. Parlow flew out of the hole relieved to see that Tommy had remembered a towel.

"You can always expect the unexpected in life, good on you for remembering a towel," said Parlow laughing.

The children climbed onto Parlow's back, he took off and ascended over Mangrove Sands; the only sound was an occasional mullet jumping out of the water and the cry of a few curlews on the ground below them.

Jake was in front with his arms wrapped around Parlow. He leant forward and asked Parlow if the letter and picture he and Tommy had written had been delivered to Dino. Parlow nodded yes as he continued to fly North. "Do you think we will see Dino again?" asked Jake hopefully.

"You just never know what lies around the corner, son," replied Parlow with a smile.

(13,14,p.31) Muandik/Bunganditj Language reclamation Project, November 2012. Project book. Burrundies Aboriginal Corporation, 49 Helen Street (PO Box 2500) Mt Gambier SA 5290.

Chapter 6

A Call for Help

First-term at school was flying past and the children had many adventures to the Enchanted Sea World. Wanjee was reading fluently with the extra tuition from Wally and was now in the top reading group at school. She had kept in touch with her tribe with notes on the boomerang and knew, in time, she would reunite with her family. Jake and Maria were also topping their class particularly in Math, they knew their times tables up to 12 times, off by heart. Rhyming times tables' songs in the Enchanted Sea World helped them to remember.

Dino, however, who left the island to attend high school on the mainland, was having some problems settling in at his new school. Although Dino knew he was on the right path and could visit his sick mother in the nursing home near his school, making friends had been difficult for him.

With the support of Wally's tutoring, some rose-coloured glasses and a new way to learn, Dino was awarded Dux of the Island Primary School last year. Unfortunately, there was a group of three boys who were always in trouble and bullied other children at Dino's new school. They had started to bully Dino.

"Hey, love your rose-coloured glasses Dino, have you got a dress to match them?" The boys would taunt him and say cruel things to him every day. Although Dino's grades were very good, he was sad. He missed his friends on the island and he missed the Enchanted Sea World.

One night after completing his homework, sitting on his bed in the boarding house, he gazed sadly out the window towards the horizon. He missed his island friends and wondered what he could do about the bullies. He had ignored them but they continued to bully him. Suddenly, he remembered the medallion Parlow had given him. He'd kept it in a locked treasure chest in a drawer on his dresser.

Parlow had said, "If you need help, rub the rainbow on the medallion." Dino thought to himself and quickly opened his top drawer and took the treasure box out. He took the key that hung on a silver chain around his neck and unlocked it, carefully taking out his medallion.

Closing his eyes, he held the medallion in one hand and gently rubbed the rainbow with the other. Suddenly, Parlow appeared in his mind's eye. With his eyes still closed, he could clearly see Parlow. "Hello son, I believe you need some help," said Parlow in his wise deep voice.

"Hey Parlow, yeah it's been a bit hard for me to make friends. There are three boys who bully me every day. I have ignored them but they continue to say nasty things. I miss the island and I miss you," Dino said with a tear in his eyes.

"Mmm," Parlow pondered. "Listen sh-very carefully. People sh-who bully other people are usually victims themselves, and this makes them sh-feel angry and take it out on other people." Dino listened carefully. "Firstly, when you're feeling sh-sad, I want you to think about what sh-you do have, not what sh-you don't have. Sh-you have good friends on the island, a loving family sh-and good grades.

Secondly, I want sh-you to write something nice about each of these boys sh-on a piece of paper and leave it on their desk at sh-school without your name sh-on it. See what happens sh-and watch their reactions. Do it every day for one week.

Thirdly, your kindness can find its way sh-into their hearts, sh-you might make a positive difference in these boys lives, sh-as we made a positive difference in yours," concluded Parlow.

"What if it doesn't work?" inquired Dino. "Keep ignoring sh-them and focus on what sh-you do have and what makes sh-you happy. Stay close to caring people sh-at school and sh-you will make friends," assured Parlow.

"Thank you, Parlow," whispered Dino with a smile. Parlow faded from Dino's mind, he opened his eyes, looked at his medallion smiling and placed it carefully back into the treasure box, locking it safely in his top drawer.

It was getting late and although Dino was tired tomorrow was Friday, the last day of the school week, so he decided to write anonymous notes for the three boys. Dino sat and thought about each boy and what he had observed them doing when they weren't bullying others.

Dino thought about the first boy, Eric. Eric liked football cards and he knew all the statistics of every player so Dino wrote;

"Eric, I think you're amazing how you know all the statistics of every football player. I think you are very clever."

Then he thought about the second boy, Damo. Damo was always talking about the fish he caught, he knew the names and species of every fish in the ocean so Dino wrote;

"Damo, you could be a marine biologist, you know so much about fish. I think that is fantastic."

Then he thought about the third boy, Stevie. Stevie loved sports cars, he was very good at drawing them in detail, so Dino wrote;

"Stevie, your sports car drawings are incredible. You are a really talented drawer."

Dino put each note into his school bag and lay down on his bed with a big smile on hisface , thinking how lucky he was to have Parlow to help and guide him.

The following day, Dino got up earlier than usual so he could get to class before anyone arrived and put the notes in the boys' wooden desks.

It wasn't far to walk to his classroom from the boarding house and he could clearly see his classroom from his bedroom window. When he saw the janitor unlock his classroom door, Dino went straight down to his classroom, carefully placing the notes in the boys' desks so they were poking out and slightly visible. Then began arranging his own books preparing for his first lesson.

Students began arriving, the quietness of being alone in the classroom soon became filled with laughter and chatter. The three bullies were late as usual, mucking about and taunting students as they arrived at school. When they finally came into the classroom and the teacher ordered them to sit down, they each noticed the note poking out of their desks.

Very loudly and abruptly Stevie called out, "What's this?" with a sarcastic tone. "A love letter?"

The other boys started laughing. "As if," said Don.

"Oh Romeo," said Damo.

Stevie read his note to himself as did Eric and Damo. Stevie tore the note up, ignored what was written and called out laughing, "I must be a Romeo, hahahah."

Don also read his note and tore it up laughing, Damo read his note and pretended to tear it up, instead he stuck it into his pocket.

Dino observed the three boys' reactions and felt the idea may not have resonated with them. "Had it worked?" Dino questioned himself, but it didn't take long. Although the boys made light of their notes in front of the class when the bell rang for recess Stevie, Damo and Eric met on the oval. Dino sat down under an old oak tree, close enough to overhear what the boys were saying.

"What did your note say?" questioned Stevie. The boys discussed what was written on each of their notes.

"I wonder who wrote them?" questioned Don.

"Probably one of the girls," replied Stevie laughing. They noticed Dino sitting under the tree and began walking towards him, Stevie leading the way.

"What ya eating?" Taunted Stevie, Eric laughed but Damo appeared to stay back.

"Just a sandwich," replied Dino. "Do you want some?" offered Dino.

"Yeah," said Stevie and grabbed Dino's sandwich and started eating what was left.

Don grabbed what was left in his lunch box, "Thanks mate, don't mind if I do," said Don in a nasty tone and began eating the remainder of Dino's lunch.

Damo didn't seem to join in, he lagged hesitantly behind the other two bullies. Stevie and Eric started walking away towards another area. "Hey, you comin?" Stevie questioned Damo.

"I have to stay with the teacher on duty down here," replied Damo.

"Sucked in," Stevie replied as he and Eric laughed and walked away eating Dino's lunch.

Dino didn't mind the bullies taking his lunch, he lived at the boarding school and knew he could get more food later. He stood up from under the oak tree and walked towards Damo who had taken his note out of his pocket and was reading it.

"You do know a lot about fish," said Dino as he approached Damo.

Damo looked up in surprise, "How did...?" Then he realised who wrote the notes. "You wrote the notes, didn't you?" stated Damo.

"Yes, I did," replied Dino.

"Hey mate, I'm sorry about teasing you with the others," Damo said.

"It's okay, mate. I know you and the other boys have probably been bullied."

Damo looked to the ground sadly, his lip began quivering and a single tear trickled down his cheek landing on his shoe. "My brother," Damo murmured to Dino.

Dino put his arm around Damo, "It's okay mate, have you told anyone?" Dino questioned.

"No, I'm too scared to say anything," replied Damo with a tone of panic in his voice.

"Perhaps if we tell the teacher and she can speak with your parents about it," suggested Dino.

"Yeah maybe that could work," replied Damo quite relieved that he had told Dino.

The bell rang and the boys made their way to class together. Dino and Damo spoke with the teacher prior to the class about Damo being bullied at home. The teacher assured Damo she would arrange a meeting with his parents. This made Damo feel much happier, he was grateful for Dino's support especially after he had been bullying him.

Strangely after the class were all seated, Stevie and Eric did not return to class. The students looked puzzled when the teacher questioned them if they knew where they were. The classroom phone rang and the teacher chatted silently looking disappointed she hung up the phone and addressed the class. "It makes me very sad to inform you all that after several warnings about bullying, Stevie and Don were caught bullying one of the students' younger siblings and have now been expelled. They will not be returning to this school."

The class were shocked but also relieved, especially Damo who leant over to Dino's desk and whispered, "They bullied me into bullying others, I was scared of them," said Damo.

Dino smiled and whispered back. "You're safe now and can focus on your studies," he said with a smile.

After school, Dino was eager to contact Parlow and let him know how the note plan had worked with one of the boys. He shook hands with Damo, said goodbye and went straight to the boarding house. Clambering up the stairs like a mountain goat at full pace, he flung his bedroom door open, threw his bag onto his bed and quickly unlocked the top draw and took his medallion out of the treasure box.

He closed his eyes and began gently rubbing the rainbow, suddenly Parlow was in his mind's eye. "Hello sh-son," said Parlow.

Dino could hardly contain himself, "It worked Parlow, the note worked, well for one of them," Dino said excitedly.

"This is very good news," replied Parlow. "You sh-said it only worked for one boy?" questioned Parlow.

"Oh the other two boys were expelled for bullying," replied Dino.

Dino explained Damo's story and what he had written on his note and their plan to stop Damo from being bullied. "Well done son," replied Parlow proudly. "I didn't tell you but your medallion can do more than just visualise and contact me," said Parlow.

"REALLY?" Dino said in excited anticipation. "What else can it do?" he questioned.

"I am standing in the classroom in the Enchanted Sea World below the virtual whiteboard. Press the sh-outer edge of the medallion," instructed Parlow. Dino pressed the outer edge of the medallion and suddenly he could see Parlow through the middle of the medallion and Parlow could see Dino on the virtual whiteboard.

"Oh wow, this is amazing, like face time, hahaha." Dino laughed jumping up and down on his bed with excitement.

"You could sh-say that." Parlow laughed. "Jake, Maria and Tommy miss sh-you and you haven't met Wanjee yet. Would sh-you like to see them on medallion face time?" questioned Parlow.

"Yes! Yes! Yes! Of course, that would be epic," replied an ecstatic Dino.

"Okay Dino contact sh-me via the virtual rainbow at approximately 7.30 pm and we sh-will make it a surprise for everyone," instructed Parlow.

"Got it, 7.30 pm tonight. OOOH, this is rad," said Dino overwhelmed with the enchantment of it all.

"Sh-see you tonight," said Parlow as he slowly faded from Dino's medallion. The last time Dino felt this excited was when he went to the Enchanted Sea World for the first time. He placed his magic medallion back into the treasure box and left it on top of his dresser, ready for his surprise catch up with his friends. Dino was so excited instead of attending the mess hall for dinner, he went to the boarding house kitchen, made a sandwich and took it back to his bedroom. It seemed like an eternity to wait from 4.30 pm until 7.30 pm so Dino started on his homework, checking the clock every 5 minutes. "Time seems to go so slowly when you want it to go fast," Dino said to himself.

Meanwhile, back on the island, Tommy, Jake, Maria and Wanjee were completing their chores and preparing for their

Enchanted Sea world adventure. Tommy's grandfather noticed that Tommy had more towels to wash every week. "What's with the extra towel every week?" questioned grandpa.

Tommy had to think very quickly, "I take one to school as I get sweaty playing sport," Tommy quickly replied as he wrapped another towel around his waist under his T-shirt.

Wanjee grabbed another bag to bring food home in, it had become a weekend treat in the Pina Wali treehouse for all the children. Maria and Jake both remembered to take their boomerangs so they could practice throwing them from the top of the water slide.

Parlow arrived on Tommy's window sill at 7 pm, punctual as always. "Hello son," said Parlow as Tommy opened his window and said the code of silence floating onto Parlow's back. Once Parlow had collected all four children and flew to Mangrove Sands, gently landing on the sand near a stingray hole.

Once the children had climbed off Parlow, he didn't summon the mud crabs straight away. "Before sh-we go down to the Enchanted Sea World, I want you all to know sh-you are receiving a surprise during class time today," said Parlow whetting the children's appetite for more information.

"Tell us, Parlow, what is it? What is it?" Jake jumped up and down pleading.

"Well sh-son, it wouldn't be a surprise if I told sh-you, would it?" Parlow said, with a cheeky smile and summoned the soldier crabs, "EEEEEE."

The children were extremely excited and without any haste lined up, said their code of silence and went shooting down the tunnel into the cushioned tunnel door. When Parlow arrived and opened the tunnel door, the rainbow light hardly had time to shine through before the children ran up the golden path towards their classroom. They ran past Ibis chef calling hello as they ran past and flung the red, ruby door open, but there was no surprise to be seen anywhere.

"Parlow said there would be a surprise in class but I can't see anything," said Jake disappointedly. Parlow flew into the classroom landing in front of the children.

"All good things come to those who wait," Parlow stated with a smile.

Wally, Delilah and Pedro's bald Dugong heads appeared out of the water as the children sat down at their desks. "Good th-evening children," said Wally in his deep alto voice.

"Good evening, Wally and tutors," the children replied in a dull tone.

It was 7.25 pm and back at the boarding school, Dino could hardly wait. Sitting on the end of his bed, he rubbed the rainbow on his medallion and shut his eyes. "We are sh-nearly ready," said Parlow quietly to Dino.

"Okay, just say the word and I will press the outer edge of the medallion," said Dino in anticipation.

While Dino was waiting, Parlow instructed Wally to turn on the virtual whiteboard. Suddenly the whiteboard hovered above the pool. "This just looks like another lesson," said Tommy a little disappointed.

"Okay, NOW," Parlow instructed Dino.

Dino pressed the outer edge of his medallion and suddenly the children saw Dino on the screen and Dino could see the children. Jumping out of their seats and pointing and waving to the whiteboard, "It's Dino! It's Dino! Hi Dino," they all yelled, except Wanjee who had never met Dino.

Dino was laughing as he waved back at his friends who he could see in his medallion. "Oh Parlow, this is such a wonderful surprise," said Maria with an elevated excited voice.

Parlow asked the children to calm down so he could introduce Wanjee. "Dino, this is Wanjee, Wanjee this is Dino," said Parlow. Dino and Wanjee waved and smiled at each other.

"One at a time, you can each have a chat with Dino," instructed Parlow. Jake raised his hand first.

"Hey mate, so good to see you, did you get my note?" questioned Jake.

"Hey, yes I did, Shian delivered both yours and Tommy's notes, I hung them on my wall. Congratulations on your bravery awards, I read it in the local newspaper," replied Dino.

"Thanks, mate, the fires were pretty bad but it was really the whales and dolphins who were the true heroes," replied Jake.

Tommy raised his hand next. "Hey mate, how is high school? And how did you manage to connect with us?" a curious Tommy asked.

"Firstly, high school has had its ups and downs, but that's life. With Parlow's support, it's going well. Secondly, the medallion Parlow gave me is incredible, it allows me to contact Parlow through visualisation and do virtual time with you all in the Enchanted Sea World," replied Dino.

"That is so awesome, I can't wait until I get my medallion," replied Tommy.

Parlow gave Tommy a wise glance and said, "All good things take time, son."

Maria raised her hand. "What does your bedroom look like?" questioned Maria. "I can give you a tour with my medallion," replied Dino.

"Oh yes, yes, please," pleaded Maria.

Dino turned the medallion around and began walking around his room, pointing the face of the medallion at different items in his bedroom. "This is my dressing table with your pictures on the wall," he took two steps left, "this is my desk," then Dino pointed the medallion at the window, "and this is my window from where I can see my mother's nursing home." Dino laughed and turned the medallion around to face himself. "It's not big, but it is all I need," said Dino.

Wanjee didn't raise her hand, she didn't know what to say to someone she had never met. Dino was curious, noticing her skin was a different colour and asked Wanjee a question. "Where are you from, Wanjee?" queried Dino.

"I come from an aboriginal tribe on South Seabrooke Island," replied Wanjee shyly.

Maria wanted Dino to know how clever Wanjee was and added excitedly, "Wanjee speaks another language and has been teaching us new words and mythical aboriginal stories. She even taught us how to make a boomerang out of tree roots," said Maria proudly holding up her boomerang to show Dino.

Dino was more than impressed, he also wanted to learn a new language. "Wow, that is awesome. Do you think you could teach me a few words?" Dino asked Wanjee.

Wanjee gave Dino a cheeky smile, "Of course, Wuwu Wingga," she said.

Dino repeated the words several times before asking what it meant. "What does it mean?" Dino asked.

Wanjee began chuckling. "It means goodbye friend," she replied laughing and Dino laughed back.

Wally noticed the time was slipping away. "I think Wanjee is right, it is time to say goodbye children," Wally said in his low deep voice.

The children didn't want Dino to go. "Stay in touch," said Maria.

"Great catching up, mate," said Jake.

"Perhaps we could catch up every Friday on medallion face time?" queried Tommy, looking at Parlow and Wally with pleading eyes.

Parlow and Wally looked at each other and nodded. "I think we could allocate 10 minutes of facetime every Friday before class," stated Wally.

The children and Dino cheered and waved goodbye.

"See you next week," they all said as Dino waved and pressed the outer edge of his medallion disappearing off the virtual whiteboard.

The facetime with Dino had taken up most of the children's learning time so Wally told the children they could have the evening off and go adventuring. "Yippee," the children echoed and quickly said goodbye thanking Wally and their tutors before heading outside to their carts.

The children chatted about their facetime with Dino as they drove their carts to the Ferris wheel. They spent the following hour enjoying the rides, practising throwing their boomerangs and chatting with the enchanted sea world creatures. Wanjee attached another note to her boomerang and cast it from the top of the water slide. Today, it didn't take long for the boomerang to return, Wanjee's tribe knew that she would cast a note every Friday around the same time and were always there waiting.

The children had a wonderful day and enjoyed another delicious healthy meal courtesy of Ibis chef. Wanjee put some food in her spare bag and for the first time, the children completed their meal without a rotten egg smell. Cram had been ordered to eat his food outside, much to the relief of the children. Today had been another magical time for the children in the Enchanted Sea World. They were thrilled they could now have regular weekly contact with their buddy Dino.

Meanwhile back at the boarding school, it was late, Dino was lying on his bed with a big broad smile repeating the new aboriginal words Wanjee had taught him and thinking how wonderful it must be to speak another language. Dino's meeting with Wanjee struck a passion within him to learn more about Aboriginal culture and language.

The weekend seemed to go by quicker than any other day of the week. Dino visited his mother in the nursing home, completed all his homework, played chess and cards with some of his colleagues in the boarding house and borrowed some aboriginal books from the library.

It was Monday morning, Dino walked down the same concrete path towards his classroom with other students, as he had done every school day. However, this particular morning was quite different. For the first time all year, Dino was not bullied. Damo arrived at school and saw Dino from the school gate, he ran down the concrete path as fast as he could with his backpack thumping his back from left to right to catch up to him. "Hey mate, slow down, how was your weekend?" Dino asked Damo who was out of breath.

Breathless Damo replied, "It was the best weekend, ever. Since our teacher spoke with my parents my brother has left me alone," Damo said smiling at Dino adding, "Thanks mate."

"No problem, but you know it was you who changed things for the better by speaking out to people who care. We all need caring supportive people around us mate," concluded Dino. The boys walked into class with a sense of unity and empowerment that comes when you feel safe and protected from bullies.

Chapter 7

Bush Potions

The year was passing quickly, there were many trips to the enchanted sea world, with new experiences and changes throughout the year. Dino was enjoying school and had made many friends including Damo. Tommy and Maria had experienced a school camp that only grade six has the privilege of attending. Both of them had grown at least 5cm taller and everyone noticed Tommy's voice was becoming deeper. Wanjee tolerated her alcoholic foster parents and continued to keep in touch with her tribe. She was happy to discover that her parents were much healthier now and planned on returning to South Seabrooke Island at the end of the year. Jake was doing well at school and had taken up playing the guitar and drums.

The children had regular Friday evening facetime with Dino who was becoming well-read on aboriginal culture, often surprising Wanjee with various indigenous phrases he had learnt.

This particular Thursday after school the children rode their bikes home together except Jake who decided to race Wanjee back to her house and take a shortcut back home.

"C'mon, race ya home," Jake challenged Wanjee.

Wanjee gave Jake a challenging grin. "You wanna be beaten?" she said with a laugh.

They both gripped their bicycle handles, stood up pushing their heels down hard on the pedals yelling back at Tommy and Maria, "See you tomorrow," and both Wanjee and Jake took off down the concrete footpath leaving Tommy and Maria laughing.

"I bet Wanjee beats him again." Tommy laughed.

Jake knew all the short cuts but Wanjee's long legs peddled like a wind turbine at full speed. She reached the turn off to her street within a few minutes, skidding around the corner she pushed the bike forward as hard as she could go for the final 100 metres, almost crashing into her front gate. She heard a rustle in the bush and Jake tore out of the bushes covered in twigs, cobwebs and dirt.

"I did ask ya if you wanna be beaten." Wanjee laughed.

Jake was breathless, "I got caught in a bunch of twines," replied Jake gasping for air.

"Come and get some water from the outdoor hose," urged Wanjee, pulling twigs off Jake's back.

As Jake gulped the water streaming out of the hose his eyes were drawn up towards a painted pole leaning against the end of the house. "What's that?" Jake asked wiping the water from his mouth.

"It's a didgeridoo," replied Wanjee.

"Where did you get it from?" queried Jake.

"I made it," Wanjee replied as she picked up the didgeridoo, inhaled some air, put her mouth over the top of it blowing out a musical sound Jake had never heard before.

"Wow, that is awesome," said Jake highly impressed with this musical instrument. "Can I have a go?" asked Jake enthusiastically.

"Sure, but it takes some practice and technique," replied Wanjee.

Wanjee handed Jake the didgeridoo, he inhaled air and blew hard, but nothing happened.

"Hahaha, I told you it takes practice, I will show you," said Wanjee. She explained to Jake how you must tighten your lips as if your smiling and not allow any air to escape, making a small hole between your lips, blow your cheeks out like a puffa fish and blow into it. Jake attempted the technique and managed to get a small sound out.

Jake was intrigued by this instrument. "What does your tribe use them for?" questioned Jake.

"We use them for tribal celebrations where we dance and paint our bodies, we call them corroborees," replied Wanjee.

"Oh I wish I had one of these to practice on," Jake said impressed by the instrument.

"I can show you how to make one in the Enchanted Sea World tomorrow night," replied Wanjee.

"Really? That would be excellent," Jake replied excitedly.

The following day when the children arrived at school, but before Tommy could ask who won the bike race, Jake looked at Tommy and said, "Yep, Wanjee won. But guess what else I discovered?" He said excitedly. Tommy and Maria tilted their heads curiously. "Wanjee made a didgeridoo and she is going to show us how to make one tonight in the enchanted sea world," said Jake lowering his voice so no one heard. Tommy and Maria wanted to squeal with excitement but just jumped up and down clapping their hands.

"This is going to be so much fun. See you later," said Tommy and Maria as they went into class.

The day passed quickly. When the afternoon bell rang, the children all met at the school gates and rode home together, chatting about their new adventure making didgeridoos with Wanjee that evening. They all said goodbye and went home to complete their homework and chores to be ready for Parlow.

Tommy remembered to wrap a towel around his waist before getting into bed with his ingot, Wanjee stuffed a spare bag into her jeans pocket and Maria and Jake took their ingots from their secret hiding places and climbed into bed excited for the evening ahead.

As Tommy lay in bed listening to the sound of noisy curlews and the occasional tropical green frog in the drainpipe, he heard the familiar swoosh and thud on his window sill as Parlow landed precisely on time.

"Hey Parlow," said Tommy affectionately. "Shamang, Shamoose, Kabang, Kaboose," said Tommy holding his ingot and floating effortlessly onto Parlow's back. Parlow pushed off the window sill spreading his large wingspan. He then picked up all the children who appeared very excited tonight.

"What have sh-you all got planned after tutoring tonight?" Parlow said as he flew towards Mangrove Sands.

"Wanjee is going to show us how to make a Didgeridoo," Jake replied in a high pitch tone.

"Well, that sh-sounds interesting," replied Parlow who already knew what they had planned.

They landed gently on Mangrove Sands near a large stingray hole and Parlow called the soldier crabs, "EEEEEEE," Parlow's deep voice echoed along the beach. Thousands of little soldier crabs scampered across the sand and began their mission of borrowing a tunnel to the Enchanted Sea World.

Each of the children repeated their code of silence as they hovered over the stingray hole and shot down the tunnel one after the other. Standing back against the walls to allow Parlow to fly down and into the pillow attached to the tunnel door.

Parlow opened the door and in shone the rainbow light onto the children. "Hello, Warrajamba," (rainbow serpent), the children all said at once as they passed through the door and into the Enchanted Sea World.

"I can't wait to tell Dino about the Didgeridoo," stated Jake excitedly walking with a hop in his step up the glittering golden path towards the shell castle.

The children entered the castle, saying hello to Cram and Ibis chef, busy as always, preparing for the children's delicious healthy meal later.

When they entered the classroom, their Dugong tutors were waiting for them with Dino on the virtual screen. "Hi Dino mate," the children said as they sat at their desks.

"Hi Wingga," (Hello Friends), replied a well-read Dino.

"Wow, you're getting pretty good with my tribal language," said Wanjee impressed.

"Thank you Wanjee, yes I've been doing a lot of reading on aboriginal culture and language over the past few weeks," replied Dino.

"Guess what Wanjee is going to teach us today?" Jake said excitedly to Dino.

"What?" queried Dino.

"She is going to teach us how to make a didgeridoo," replied Jake, keen to share his news.

"I read in one of my books that you make didgeridoos out of termite eaten tree trunks," replied a well-read Dino.

"Yes, that is correct," replied Wanjee.

After 10 minutes of chatting with Dino, the children said goodbye, "Wuwu Wingga," they all said.

"Wuwu wingga," replied Dino and pressed the outer edge of his medallion and disappeared from the virtual screen. Just as Dino disappeared, the 11 times table song came on and the children began singing.

1x11 = 11 feels like heaven
2x11 = 22 shoo fly shoo
3x11 = 33 whales at sea
4x11 = 44 and there's more
5x11 = 55 jig and jive
6x11 = 66 sherbet mix
7x11 = 77 cheese and devon
8x11 = 88 you're my mate
9x11 = 99 all is fine
10x11 = 110 do it again
11x11 = 122 Bigaloo
12x11 = 132 this is new

Wally turned the virtual whiteboard off and commended the children on the progress they were making with their times tables. "Now, I would like to learn how you make a didgeridoo," said Wally smiling at Wanjee. "I would th-like Wanjee to stand up and tell th-all of us how to make a didgeridoo th-and what it is used for. While Wanjee is explaining this, I would like the resth-of you to take notes," instructed Wally.

The children were eager to hear how they were going to make a didgeridoo. Wanjee stood up in front of her friends and began explaining as the others began writing.

"Well, first you have to find termite eaten eucalyptus trunks. Then you tap the trunk to check and see if it is hollow. Then you use a stone axe to cut the trunk. Usually, you must soak the trunk in water for one day but we will only have a short time. Then you must prise out any bits inside the hollow trunk with a stick. Lastly, you must hold the trunk under-water to see if there are any air bubbles," Wanjee concluded.

"What if there are air bubbles?" questioned Jake.

"It means there are holes in the didgeridoo and they must be covered over with beeswax," replied Wanjee. **(15)**

Wally thanked Wanjee for sharing this cultural knowledge as the children were busy writing all the instructions down. "Just before you sit down, can th-you explain what you use the didgeridoo for?" asked Wally.

Wanjee went on to explain that the didgeridoo is an aboriginal musical instrument played at aboriginal tribal ceremonies called 'Corroborrees' where there is cultural dance and celebrations. "Perhaps th-we could have a Corroboree at the end of the year," suggested Wally.

"Oh really, that would be lovely," replied Wanjee.

The children were dismissed from class and quickly made their way out to their carts on the search for some termite eaten eucalyptus tree trunks. "We need to look in a shaded damp spot," instructed Wanjee. The children found some nice dense bush close to the shore at the foot of the water slide. They parked their carts and began walking into the bush. "Hang on," Wanjee said to her friends, "we need to find some sharp-edged rocks first." The children followed Wanjee and began looking for rocks along the shoreline.

Once they had all found a sharp-edged rock, they followed Wanjee into the dense damp forest. Mildew, moss and mould covered most of the forest trees and rocks. "Here is a good one," announced Wanjee, as she studied a large termite eaten eucalyptus tree trunk, tapping it. "This one is perfect, not too thick and looks almost completely hollow," she said excitedly.

Three more termite-eaten trunks stood a few metres apart. Wanjee checked, tapped and studied each one. "These ones are perfect," said Wanjee who began chopping the base of the trunk with her sharp-edged rock. Maria, Tommy and Jake watched what Wanjee was doing and with their sharp-edged rocks began chopping at their tree trunks.

Wanjee had cut through hers, Maria was almost through, and as Tommie's trunk came crashing down there was an almighty scream from Jake. The children turned around to see Jake rolling around groaning on the ground, holding his knee to his chest, covered in blood. "Oh no what happened?" Maria cried out as they all ran over to Jake.

"OW, OW, OW, I missed the tree and put the rock straight into my knee," cried out Jake.

Wanjee started collecting termite dust, ran to the shoreline and collected some mud and with a large cocos leaf and a stick combined the dust and mud and began mixing it together.

"What are you doing? Can't you see Jake is in agony?" said Maria quite concerned.

"This is an aboriginal remedy to stop infection," replied Wanjee. "Cup your hands and collect some saltwater and pour it over Jake's wound," instructed Wanjee. The children ran down to the shoreline and each of them cupped their hands and ran back to Jake still holding his knee to his chest.**(16)**

"Jake, let go of your knee, I promise this will help," Wanjee assured him. Jake let go of his knee and the children tipped the saltwater directly onto the wound which made Jake scream again as it stung. "It's okay Jake, now the wound is clean, I will dress it with this paste," said Wanjee. Jake reluctantly allowed Wanjee to dress his wound. Carefully, using one finger, Wanjee scooped up some paste mix and gently spread it over the wound. Jake calmed down as the paste stopped the stinging and made it feel much better.

"Thanks, guys, it does feel better. I reckon I can cut my tree trunk down now," said Jake determined to make his didgeridoo.

"No no no," replied Tommy. "You sit there, I will finish it off for you," said Tommy.

"Thanks, mate," replied Jake who was relieved he didn't have to use that wretched rock again. Tommy took his rock and with one large hit, Jake's tree trunk came crashing down. "Would you like me to finish yours?" Tommy asked Maria who was still sitting with Jake.

"Yes, please," replied Maria. Once all the trunks were down, Wanjee instructed the others that the trunks needed to be soaked in water. Jake got up off the ground, using Maria's shoulder to lift himself up. He hopped over to his tree trunk and put his mouth over the end pursing his lips tightly. A little deep sound popped out the end of the trunk. "Hahaha, it's not ready to use yet." Wanjee laughed as she looked for a rock water pool they could soak the trunks in.

Meanwhile, Jake continued blowing and trying to make a sound come out of his trunk. "It sounds like Cram after he has eaten." Tommy and Maria laughed.

"Here, I found a water hole wide enough for the trunks," called out Wanjee. The children took their trunks over to the water hole. Just as the children lay the trunks in the water, the children heard a deafening croaking sound and lots of small croaks echoing through the valley. The children looked up and sitting on a very large eucalyptus branch above their heads was a gigantic tropical green frog, the size of a baby elephant. He was so big his slimy green body sagged over the swaying branch. Each of his foot pads was as large as the children's heads. Hundreds of small green tree frogs were scattered and attached to the tree below him.

"Oh no, it's Tiddalick," said Wanjee in shock. The giant frog looked at Wanjee and smiled.

"Haha, cr-no I am not Tiddalick, he is my cousin, my name is Toddalick, I am the cr-healing frog and I cr-heard the sound of a didgeridoo call so I cr-came."

The children looked puzzled. "That must have been Jake making sounds from his trunk," stated Tommy. "Who is Tiddalick?" Tommy asked Wanjee. The children all sat on the grass under the shade of the trees as Wanjee began to tell the aboriginal dreamtime story of Tiddelick the greedy frog.

The children listened with intent and anticipation as Wanjee began the story. "There was once a very greedy frog called Tiddalick, he was the largest frog in the world. One warm morning he woke up very thirsty and started drinking the freshwater. He didn't stop drinking until the billabong was dry.

There was no water left for the other animals and they knew Tiddalick was the culprit. The animals needed to come up with a plan to get their water back. After much thinking, they decided to make Tiddalick laugh so he would spill all the water out of his mouth and back into the billabong.

The Echidna tried to make him laugh by rolling herself up in a ball and rolling down the bank. The Emu and Kangaroo laughed but not Tiddalick.

Wombat tried to make him laugh by dancing on one leg until he fell over in the dirt. Others laughed but not Tiddalick.

The Kookaburra tried to make him laugh by telling her funniest story. Others laughed but not Tiddalick.

Finally, the last one to try was the snake. The snake wriggled around on the ground tying itself into a knot. The knot was so tight the snake could not get free from herself and she was stuck. Tiddalick watched the snake struggling and let out a small chuckle which turned into a rourkess laugh making Tiddalick's full belly of water come gushing out of his mouth and back into the billabong.

The animals drank from the billabong happy to have some water again, and that is the story of Tiddalick, the greedy frog," concluded Wanjee. **(17)**

Jake looked up at Tiddalick's cousin Toddalick and said, "Well I hope you don't drink the water from our billabong where we have our didgeridoos soaking."

"Hahaha, NO," replied Toddalick, "I, dear sir, am a cr-healing frog and I see your knee requires cr-healing," said Toddalick.

Jake looked down at his knee covered in bush paste and agreed it would be lovely to have it all healed.

Toddalick gave one big leap that shook the earth as his huge green slimy body thumped onto the ground.

"Come over to me," beckoned Toddalick to Jake. Jake was a little hesitant as the frog was massive but slowly approached Toddalick. "Hold your cr-knee out," instructed Toddalick. Jake held his knee towards Toddalick who extended one of his footpads and gently lowered it over Jake's knee.

The children could not believe what they were witnessing. An emerald greenish-yellow glow appeared from Toddalick's pad and surrounded Jake's sore knee while Toddalick was chanting, "Cro, Cra, Cru, Cro, Cra, Cru, I am healing you, Cro, Cra, Cru, Cro, Cra, Cru, I am healing you." After Toddalick had finished his chant, the glowing light disappeared and he lifted his giant pad off Jake's knee. The children looked, open-mouthed in surprise as Jake bent down to look at his knee. He was shocked to see there was no paste, no wound and the knee looked normal again.

"How, how, how did you do that?" questioned Jake in complete amazement.

"Hahahahah, I told cr-you I am the healing frog," replied Toddalick.

"Wow, you are awesome," the children all said and went over to Toddalick giving him a hug. "Thank you, Toddalick," said Jake in appreciation. Just then the meal bell rang out through the valley.

"We must go now," said Wanjee.

"But what about our didgeridoos?" said Jake, who was concerned to leave them soaking.

"We can ask Parlow to take them out to dry later, we will have to finish them next week," replied Wanjee.

The children thanked Toddalick again, got into their carts and drove towards the shell castle, waving to Mut and Tut turtle at the water slide and Joanna at the Ferris wheel. "See you next week," they called out to their friends.

As the children drove their carts back to the castle, Jake studied his knee, still in awe of Toddalick's magic. The children chatted about the size and magical power of Toddalick and how lucky they were to have the Enchanted Sea World.

On arrival at the castle, the children noticed Cram sitting outside chewing on a mini potato pie. "Mmm, that smells good," said Jake. Cram only made a noise and not from his mouth, the children laughed and ran inside. "I retract my words, it now smells foul." Jake laughed running inside.

Ibis had prepared another delicious meal for the children. Mango and banana smoothies, fresh garden salad, mini potato pies and a delicious sherbet cake surprise for dessert. "Oh Ibis chef, this does look delicious," said Maria inhaling the delicious aroma of fresh food as she sat at the table.

Parlow was already waiting for the children at the head of the table.

"How was your adventure?" asked Parlow.

"Well, we know you already know but I put a gash in my knee with a sharp-edged rock. Wanjee stopped the infection with an aboriginal paste and then we met Toddalick who happens to be Tiddalick's cousin and he completely healed my wound with his giant glowing footpad," summed up Jake.

"Ahhhh, so sh-you met the famous sh-healing frog Toddalick," said Parlow.

"Yes, why didn't you tell us about him?" questioned Maria.

"Everything sh-has its place and time in life, everything!" stated Parlow profoundly.

As the children were eating and chatting about their adventure, Wanjee remembered she must ask Parlow if he could remove their didgeridoos the next day. "Parlow, would you mind removing our didgeridoos from the water hole by the water slide tomorrow? They need one whole day to soak and will be dry by the time we come back next week," said Wanjee.

"Of course I sh-can," replied Parlow. "I'm looking forward to hearing sh-you all play the didgeridoo, but I'm afraid sh-your time is up and sh-we must get you home," stated Parlow.

The children took their plates to the kitchen, thanking Ibis chef for the lovely meal. Wanjee filled her bag with a few potato pies and the leftover sherbet cake.

"It's certainly pleasant finishing a meal without Cram in here," stated Tommy. But just as he opened the castle front door a very nasty smell drifted past them.

"Oh Cram, you are disgusting," said the children running down the glittering golden path towards the tunnel.

"Squawk, squawk," Cane screeched out agreeing with the children and flying with them as they ran away from the ghastly smell.

One by one the children lined up as the whales took their tilted positions in the water facing their blowholes towards the tunnel. Tommy went first and was shot up as the water hit him,

Maria went next, Jake then Wanjee. They all landed in the wet sand and wiped themselves dry with Tommy's towel. Parlow flew out of the tunnel and the children climbed on his back.

As Parlow ascended up into the moonlit sky, Jake was at the front, he leaned forward with his face pressed up against Parlow's feathery cheek and said, "I still cannot believe the magical frog and his amazing healing powers."

Parlow replied, "Son, magic can be found where and when you least expect it in life."

Jake hugged Parlow affectionately knowing that Parlow was the wisest of all living things he had ever known.

(15,16) www.australiangeographic.com.au
(17) http://dreamtime.net.au/tiddalick-the-frog/

Chapter 8

Toxic Waste

The children had another good week at school as the third term was nearing an end before the holidays. Wanjee had reached the top reading level in her class with all the extra tutoring from Wally. Maria and Tommy had become very good school leaders and were preparing for high school orientation. Jake was top of his class in Math and had joined a school band playing lead guitar but what he really wanted to do was master the didgeridoo.

It was Friday and the children were excited to get to the Enchanted Sea World and finish their didgeridoos. After they all rode home and did their chores they prepared for the evening. Tommy grabbed a towel and his ingot, Wanjee made sure she had a spare bag and took her boomerang as she didn't have time to send a message last week. Jake and Maria made sure they had their ingots ready and lay in bed waiting for Parlow to land on their window sill.

The children waited but Parlow didn't arrive on Tommy's window sill at 7 pm. *What had happened?* Thought Tommy. *Parlow is always on time.* The others were wondering the same thing as they lay waiting. It was now 7.30 pm when Tommy heard the swoosh of Parlow's large wings landing on his window sill.

Tommy quickly opened the window. "Is everything okay?" questioned Tommy curious to know why Parlow was late.

"Not really sh-son, when I checked your didgeridoos today I found a black toxin sh-had dried all over the didgeridoos and when I looked into the billabong there was a black film floating sh-on the surface. The whales alerted sh-me to an environmental disaster. The hill sh-at Junkyard Well was so full of waste, it has caused the hill to split causing toxins to seep sh-into the sea and now into the Enchanted Sea world. We must be quick, son." Tommy quickly said his code of silence and floated onto Parlow's back and they flew directly to Maria's, Jake's and Wanjee's. Parlow told them to get onto his back quickly there had been a disaster.

Tommy explained to the others on the way to the enchanted sea world what had happened. "Oh no that is terrible," exclaimed Maria. "I hope the sea creatures and the sea world are not damaged," she said extremely concerned.

"Do you have a plan?" called out Jake to Parlow.

"Yes son, we have a plan, I'll explain when we get to the Enchanted Sea World."

Parlow glided onto Mangrove Sands and quickly summoned the soldier crabs. The children didn't hesitate to get off and go down the tunnel as quickly as the crabs had dug the tunnel. They stood back waiting for Parlow who flew down soon after. They could not waste a minute and quickly walked up the golden path.

"I want sh-you children to get in sh-your carts and go straight to sh-your didgeridoos, I had the bees bring wax for the mouthpiece. I want you to make as much sh-sound out of the didgeridoos as sh-you can," instructed Parlow. "I will meet sh-you at the bottom of the water slide," said Parlow. The children didn't ask any questions they all jumped into their carts and made their way to the bottom of the water slide. When the children arrived they found their didgeridoos all dried out and leaning against a large eucalyptus tree. Jake picked his up and noticed one of the hollow ends had been sealed with beeswax.

The children all held their didgeridoos to their mouths. Wanjee instructed them to purse their lips leaving a small hole in the middle of their lips and blow. The children all blew into the didgeridoos, Maria and Tommy had difficulty getting much sound out but kept trying. Wanjee and Jake were making a lovely long, loud humming sound coming out of their didgeridoos. Just as Parlow flew down to the children they all spotted Toddalick hopping heavily down the water slide hill with hundreds of little green frogs hopping twice as fast to keep up with him until they were face to face with the children and Parlow.

"Cr-hello children, what can I do for cr-you?" said Toddalick in a slow deep voice.

"We have sh-an environmental disaster and I believe sh-you can fix the problem," said Parlow explaining that the hill on the side of Junkyard Well had ruptured and toxins were seeping into the ocean and had entered the Enchanted Sea World. Many of the sea creatures were already getting sick.

"I believe I can be cr-of service," replied Toddalick. "Jump cr-on my pads," he instructed the children. Tommy, Jake, Maria and Wanjee lay their didgeridoos down on the grass and carefully stepped onto Toddalick's huge green pads. Very carefully Toddalick lifted his pad and placed the children on his back. "You cr-will stick like glue cr-up there," Toddalick said to the children.

"I can't move, it's like slimy superglue up here," said Jake.

"Hang on," said Toddalick as he leapt forward up the hill with hundreds of little tropical frogs hopping behind.

Parlow flew ahead. "I'll meet you there," called out Parlow. The children couldn't wave as their hands were stuck like glue to Toddalicks back.

It didn't take many giant leaps before Toddalick was at the entrance of Ollie and Archie's cave. They were all standing at the front entrance including the babies who looked very pale.

"Hi guys, ph-we know what has happened, the babies ph-are now sick from the toxic waste. We must stay ph-with them. Please go through Toddalick," urged Ollie. Toddalick was so huge he could barely fit into the cave and was unable to hop as he would have squashed the children on the roof of the cave. He carefully walked as fast as he could through the cave. The children bent their heads down so they didn't hit the roof. When Toddalick and the other frogs hit the sand on South Seabrooke Island they leapt as fast as they could along the white sandy shore towards Junkyard well.

Toddalick took giant leaps in the air and came thudding back down spraying sand into the water and leaving a trail of sand dust behind him. With his giant leaps, he was near the southern tip of the island in no time. The children could see Parlow standing on the sand in the distance and keen to get off what felt like a camel ride at full speed. They could clearly see a stream of black toxic substance oozing from the hillside of the junkyard well and spilling into the ocean creating artistic swirls of black liquid as if someone had spilt a huge black ink well into the water.

Once Toddalick had stopped at the tip of South Seabrooke Island, he dipped one of his large green pads into the ocean and cast a spray of water up over the children who suddenly loosened from the sticky glue and came sliding down Toddalick's back tumbling onto the soft white sand below.

Parlow announced that he must go and do one more job. "I must sh-go and sh-seek out the humpback whales. You children sh-stay here," announced Parlow as he ascended up into the sky. Toddalick asked the children to stand back and gave one large thump on the sand with his front pad. The little green frogs all hopped onto Toddalick, he was covered in little tiny green tree frogs. He took one step backwards and with one ginormous leap he flew over the ocean landing on the top of Junkyard Well.

"OH WOW," exclaimed Jake.

"That was amazing," stated Maria.

"Awesome," both Wanjee and Tommy said together. As they watched from the shores of the island they saw the little frogs all collecting rocks and climbing back onto Toddalick.

Then Toddalick positioned his body over the split on the side of the hill with one pad on either side of the gap, he placed one pad over the top of where the split began and suddenly a bright greenish-yellow glow of light penetrated into the crack as he chanted, "Cra, Cro, Cru, I will heal you, Cra, Cro, Cru, I will heal you."

One at a time, the little frogs placed a rock into the split as Toddalick made his way slowly down the hillside, sliding his glowing pad down the split while the frogs placed rocks into the crack. "Look Toddalick is sealing the split like a welder," said Jake in awe of this magical frog. The bottom of the hillside was under the ocean, when Toddalick reached the water he suddenly disappeared and nothing but a greenish-yellow glow came from beneath the water.

The black toxic liquid stopped seeping out of the hillside, only a black film remained on the ocean surface. Suddenly a large green head appeared out of the water on the other side. Toddalick took two giant leaps to the top of Junkyard Well with the little frogs all over him. Standing on the hill, he took one step backwards and the children could see he was about to leap across the ocean. "Stand back," yelled out Tommy as Toddalick leapt through the air landing with an enormous thump back onto South Seabrooke Island.

The children all cheered and hugged Toddalick, wiping the sand from their faces after Toddalicks landing. Then they all heard the sound of a familiar majestic singing sound. "Is that Bigaloo?" questioned Jake as a giant majestic humpback came into sight.

"Yes it is Bigaloo," stated Tommy.

Bigaloo swam around the ocean with his enormous mouth open. "Look, he is collecting the black toxic film off the ocean surface," said Maria. Bigaloo tilted his body and suddenly squirted black toxic liquid out of his blowhole and back into the junkyard well. More humpbacks arrived doing the same thing. The ocean was full of humpback whales blowing black toxic liquid back into Junkyard Well.

Parlow was flying above the whales before landing next to the children and Toddalick. Bigaloo let out another majestic singing sound and swam away. "I wonder where he is going?" questioned Wanjee. The ocean was almost completely free from the toxic waste when Bigaloo reappeared with something amazing on the end of his large tail.

"Look, Bigaloo has a boulder on his tail," yelled out Jake.

Bigaloo turned his body towards Junkyard well and with all his strength he flipped the boulder up into the air, over Junkyard well onto an adjoining hillside. The boulder crashed into the top of the hill creating an enormous crater which made the waste from the Junkyard well spill over into it.

"What an amazing creature, Bigaloo has released the pressure from excessive waste in Junkyard well and has made another holding well for the waste," stated Tommy.

By the time the pod of whales had stopped squirting black toxic liquid out of their blowholes, there was not a drop of pollution to be seen in the ocean. Bigaloo gave out a final majestic singing sound, the school of whales also sang like a chorus of angels, flipped their large tails and gently glided back out to sea.

The children decided they would rather fly back with Parlow rather than go on what felt like a bumpy camel ride on Toddalick. "Thank sh-you Toddalick, you have sh-saved the ocean and the sh-sea creatures," said Parlow gratefully.

"My pleasure," replied Toddalick who took one giant leap with hundreds of green frogs covering him, leaving nothing but a sand storm behind him. The children covered their faces from the sand and one at a time said the code of silence. They hovered onto Parlow's back and flown back to their carts at the bottom of the water slide where their didgeridoos and Wanjee's boomerang lay on the ground.

The children climbed off Parlow's back just as the meal bell rang. "Oh drat," stated Jake. "We didn't get to finish our didgeridoos or chat with Dino."

"No, but the ocean and creatures have been saved. In sh-times of a crisis sh-we must sometimes make sh-certain sacrifices," stated Parlow.

While Parlow was talking, Wanjee quickly scribbled a charcoal note and attached it to her boomerang casting it over to South Seabrooke Island. "I know I won't have time to receive a reply but I just had to send a note this week," said Wanjee.

The children rested their didgeridoos up against a eucalyptus tree and began driving their carts back to the castle when they saw several humpback whales in the Enchanted Sea World, scooping up toxic black liquid that had escaped in. The whales squirted it out of their blowholes into beeswax barrels. The bees miraculously sealed the barrels when they were full and the Whistling Kites were flying the barrels and dumping them in Junkyard Well.

"What a clever bunch of creatures," stated Maria in awe of how clever and magical the creatures of the Enchanted Sea World were.

The children arrived at the castle rather hungry after their adventure. Ibis Chef had prepared a lovely feast of delicious food including; Pumpkin and spinach pasta, potato patties, fresh bread rolls and a huge bowl of fresh fruit salad and cupcakes with strawberry, mango and pineapple icing and a little handmade chocolate resembling each fruit was placed on the top of the icing.

The children piled the food onto their plates and hardly spoke, they were so hungry and busy eating the delicious food Ibis Chef had made. After they had finished eating, Wanjee put as many leftover cupcakes into her bag as she could fit and a few leftover bread rolls. "Thank you, Ibis Chef," the children said as they took their plates to the kitchen.

"That was delicious," said Wanjee who was looking much healthier from all the healthy food Ibis had been making all year.

Ibis Chef nodded his long black beak in appreciation as the children made their way to the tunnel with Parlow. "Tutoring as normal next week," Parlow said to the children.

"Fingers crossed! You never know what life might throw at you from day to day," replied Tommy.

"So true, but it is the sh-way you deal with sh-things that are thrown at sh-you that is important," replied Parlow. "You sh-all stepped up and helped to sh-save the environment. You left what sh-you preferred to do, followed instructions and sh-did as you were asked, I am very proud of sh-you all, you show great maturity," commented Parlow.

The children smiled and felt proud of their contribution. "We will complete our didgeridoos next week and hopefully my boomerang will be back," said Wanjee.

One by one the children stood in front of the tunnel lining up with the humpback whales who squirted water out of their blowholes shooting the children up the tunnel and back onto Mangrove Sands. They all wiped themselves dry with Tommy's towel as Parlow flew out of the tunnel landing next to them. Climbing onto Parlow's back, he flew the children home through the gentle warm evening breeze until next week's visit to the Enchanted Sea World.

The following day the children met on their bikes at Wanjee's house, as they did every Saturday before heading to their cubby house to snack on the delicious left over's Wanjee always took after every meal at the Sea Shell Castle.

When they arrived at Wanjee's home, the children noticed Wanjee on the ground drawing in the dirt. "Hey Wanjee, what are you drawing?" questioned Jake intrigued at the circles within circles that Wanjee had drawn with her fingers in the red soil.

"It's an aboriginal symbol that represents a campsite and a waterhole," replied Wanjee still drawing.

"Wow, you have your own symbolic art?" questioned Jake, impressed with all that Wanjee knew.

"Yes we do, I can show you some more symbolic art at the cubby house," replied Wanjee standing up and climbing on her pink bike with the bag of cupcakes in her hand.

"Race ya," yelled out Jake who got a head start on Wanjee who quickly gave the bag of cupcakes to Maria and sped off calling back to Tommy and Maria,

"I'll meet you there."

Tommy and Maria laughed. "She will beat him again." Tommy laughed as he and Maria gently rode towards the cubby house.

Meanwhile, Jake was peddling as fast as his legs would take him. He felt confident, with a slight head start, he would beat Wanjee this time. But as he came tearing out of the bush, red dust flying everywhere he was shocked to see Wanjee standing with her pink bike next to the cubby house. "How did you do that?" said Jake totally surprised. "Was it some kind of magic?" Jake asked her, gasping for air.

"No." Wanjee laughed. "My long legs take me twice as fast as you," replied Wanjee as Tommy and Maria came into sight riding down the dirt track towards them.

"I told you she would beat him," said Tommy, laughing.

"You need to grow longer legs," said Maria with a chuckle.

"Yeah, yeah, c'mon let's have some of those delicious cupcakes," said Jake, diverting the attention away from the loss and onto the cupcakes. The children rested their bikes up against the treehouse and climbed up the anchor rope ladder into the cubby house.

Wanjee opened the bag and they all took a cupcake each. "Mmm, these are delicious," said Tommy with a mouthful of cupcake.

"Ibis chef is the best," said Maria. As they were eating, Jake noticed several kangaroos had gathered at the base of their cubby house.

"Look, the roos must want some food," said Jake.

"They can eat grass," replied Tommy, "processed food is not good for animals," he said.

The floor of the cubby house was made of planks of wood. A thin layer of red, blown dust, blown in by the wind, was always present on the floor. Wanjee sat on the floor and began drawing with her finger in the dust, what looked like, fishing hooks parallel to each other. "Why are you drawing fishing hooks in the dust?" questioned Jake.

"Haha, they are not fishing hooks, they are symbols, they represent kangaroo tracks," replied Wanjee. **(18)**

Tommy, Jake and Maria sat down on the floor with Wanjee and began to copy her aboriginal symbolic art. They drew the symbolic campsite, the kangaroo tracks and Wanjee showed them how to draw the representation of a woman and a man.

Within half an hour, the entire cubby house floor was covered with symbolic aboriginal artwork. "Hey, I have a good idea, why don't we paint these symbols all over the cubby house and make a sign that says 'Pina Wali' and we can hang it on the front of the tree?" stated Jake. Wanjee showed her friends how dirt rocks work well as a drawing tool so they all found a dirt rock and began decorating the cubby inside and out with symbolic artwork and several dot pictures of the rainbow serpent.

Wanjee had found a lovely piece of driftwood and wrote 'Pina Wali' on it with her dirt rock on it. They all stood back with their hands covered in red soil, impressed and proud of their new look aboriginal Pina Wali. Wanjee held the sign up. "Where do you think we should put this?" she asked.

"I have some string in my pocket," said Jake pulling a long piece of string out of his pocket. "The driftwood has two holes on either side, we can hang it on that branch at the entrance to the cubby," said Jake.

The others approved and they hung the Pina Wali sign up. As they stood back admiring their work, Tommy said to Wanjee, "You never know what life may throw at you. You have taught us so much about your aboriginal culture that I almost feel I've known you all my life as if your culture has always been a part of me."

Wanjee smiled and replied, "Well you kinda have, although we look different and have different ways, we all live in the same place and we are all human."

(18) https://www.aboriginalart.com.au

Chapter 9

Corroboree

Every week was going by so quickly and this week was no exception. It was the middle of the final school term. Tommy and Maria were preparing for high school orientation, both would be attending different high schools on the mainland and commute every day. During one class, their teacher gave them bus and ferry timetables and made all the students locate the connecting school bus they would need to catch after they got off the ferry.

Although Tommy and Maria were attending different high schools, they would be catching the same bus which made them very happy. Tommy and Maria talked a lot about high school and what it would be like, both saying they felt excited but also a little nervous. Wanjee talked a lot about going home to her tribe as soon as her parents were home from the hospital.

Jake was busy with his music at school and looking forward to his final year at primary school.

It was Friday afternoon, The school bell rang and children dispersed into the schoolyard meeting their parents and carers. As Tommy, Maria, Jake and Wanjee rode home on their bikes, Jake was singing a song the children had never heard before. "What is that song called?" asked Wanjee.

"It's my own song, it's called 'Mangrove Sands and You'; I wrote it at school," replied Jake and he continued singing;

> *"Lonely nights I cried to sleep,*
> *Until my friends, I did meet*
> *Good food, Pina Wali time,*
> *racing bikes, life is fine.*
> *Mangrove Sands, Friday and you,*
> *now I'm never ever blue.*
> *Learning, driving, flying high,*
> *one by one we say goodbye*
> *Although we will soon part,*
> *always together*
> *in my heart.*
> *Mangrove Sands, Friday and you,*
> *now I'm never ever blue."*

As Jake sang his song, Wanjee, Tommy and Maria began singing the chorus with Jake. The children stopped their bikes when they reached the corner of Jake's street. "See you tonight," said Jake waving, as he rode down his street singing his song.

The children rode home impressed with Jake's ability to write and play music. "We could learn to play the song with our didgeridoos when we finish them," said Wanjee as she waved goodbye to Tommy and Maria crossing the road. "Great idea," Maria called back.

That evening after the children had all completed the chores, they prepared for their evening in the Enchanted Sea World, towel, ingots, spare bag for food and lay waiting in bed for Parlow. Tommy was humming Jake's song when he heard the familiar '*swoosh*' of Parlow's wings and the thud of Parlow's feet landing on his window sill. "Right on time, as always," Tommy said to himself with a smile.

Tommy opened his window giving Parlow an affectionate hug, "Hey Parlow, good to see you, Kabang, Kaboose, Shamang, Shamoose," said Tommy holding his ingot and floating onto Parlow's feathery white back.

"We sh-have another surprise for sh-you tonight," announced Parlow as he pushed off Tommy's window sill.

"Tell me, tell me," pleaded Tommy.

"Hahaha, sh-you know it wouldn't be a sh-surprise if I told sh-you." Parlow laughed.

"You're a big tease," said Tommy laughing.

Parlow picked up the other children as Tommy announced to them one by one that Parlow had a surprise for them tonight. "And he won't tell us anymore until we get to the Enchanted Sea World," Tommy informed the others.

"You're a big tease," they all told Parlow. Parlow laughed, he enjoyed keeping the children in suspense and watching the children's excited anticipation for surprises.

Parlow was soon descending towards Mangrove Sands gliding down and landing gently onto the soft sand. "EEEEE," Parlow called and 1000s of soldier crabs scurried across the sand digging and lining the tunnel to the Enchanted Sea World.

The children were eager to get to class as quickly as possible to discover their surprise. They quickly said the code of silence before shooting down the tunnel one at a time and landing into the cushioned door. Parlow came flying down after them and into the door. Just to keep the children in suspense he took his time to open the door. "Oh come on, Parlow, open the door, open the door," all the children begged him.

"All good sh-things come to sh-those who wait," said Parlow laughing at the children's excitement.

Parlow slowly opened the tunnel door, the rainbow light shined in and the children raced up the glittering golden path. Parlow slowly followed the children having a quiet chuckle to himself.

The children ran past the dining area, up the slate corridor floor like a stampede of elephants and flung open the red ruby classroom door. To their surprise, all they saw were their didgeridoos leaning up against their desks.

"Well that was nice of Parlow to bring our didgeridoos to the classroom, but it's not really a surprise," said Jake in a disappointed tone.

"Oh you know Parlow, he always keeps us waiting with surprises," commented Tommy. They all agreed and sat at their desks when Parlow casually walked into the classroom with a wry smile on his face.

"See I told you, he is playing games with us," said Tommy to the others with a little chuckle.

"Hahaha, sh-you know me sh-too well," replied Parlow. "You sh-are right, there is another sh-surprise, but…" and Parlow was interrupted by all four children who said in unison, "All good things come to those who wait."

Parlow laughed and Wally, Delilah and Pedro popped their heads out of the pool, the virtual whiteboard came on and there was Dino staring at them with a big broad smile.

"Hey guys, what have you been up to?" questioned Dino. One by one, they each took turns describing their latest adventures, Toddalick, Junkyard well and the didgeridoos they had made.

Dino enjoyed his Friday catch up and had settled into his new school and made several friends since the bullies had been expelled. His grades were top of the class and he still wanted to become a marine biologist. "Only one term left of year seven and then only three years left of high school before I can attend University," Dino said with maturity.

"Wow, university," Wanjee said highly impressed with Dino's ambitious future. "It seems a long way off for me," replied Wanjee.

"It passes quickly so enjoy your time and make it count," replied Dino wisely.

Wanjee had never spoken about anything she might like to do when she was older but Dino had made her think about it. "I'm not exactly sure what I want to do when I'm older but I do know I would like to be an advocate for our indigenous culture," she said proudly.

"That sounds wonderful," stated Wally who was listening, as he did, with intent, at the children's conversation.

"It is time to say goodbye to Dino now children," Wally announced.

The children said goodbye and sat waiting for their next instruction. "As you can see, Parlow kindly flew all your didgeridoos back to the classroom this week. He also kindly collected some coloured clay in the palm leaves sitting in the corner over there, wally pointed to the palm leaves. You can paint them during your class time," said Wally.

"Awesome," said Jake excited to finish his didgeridoo.

After virtual time with Dino and receiving their classroom instruction, the children had forgotten about the surprise Parlow had planned. They each took a palm leaf and a stick and began painting indigenous symbolic art on their didgeridoos.

Both Wanjee and Maria painted the rainbow serpent winding from the top to the bottom of the didgeridoo using dots to outline the serpent. Jake painted kangaroo tracks all over his and Tommy painted dot circles, small rainbow serpents and a few kangaroo tracks on his. As the children stood back admiring each other's paintings Parlow appeared with Wanjee's boomerang and as he handed it to Wanjee four whistling kites swooped past the classroom with swings attached to their legs.

The children looked at one another open-mouthed with an air of excitement and anticipation as Parlow began to explain the surprise.

"Sh-I found a bark note on the sh-boomerang, and had sh Wally looked up the translation," said Parlow. It read;

"Hi, Wanjee,
you will be pleased to know your
parents have returned to the tribe
and we invite you and your friends
to a Corroboree next Friday.
From the Moandik Tribe."

Wanjee could hardly contain her excitement, her legs were jumping up and down like a kangaroo hopping on the spot whilst she cupped her mouth with her hands so as not to explode with excitement while Parlow spoke.

Then with an enormous squeal Wanjee shouted out, "I can't believe it my parents are home, they are home, they are home. Does that mean we are going to see them now?" questioned Wanjee bursting with excitement.

"Yes sh-you are all going with the whistling kites sh-who will fly you to sh-your tribe, they are waiting for sh-you," replied Parlow with a sense of accomplishment of another successful surprise.

The children danced around the room hugging Parlow and thanking him. "We must sh-hurry as you only have a few hours, everyone sh-out to the front of the castle, the Kites are sh-waiting for you," instructed Parlow.

The children said goodbye to their tutors and paced swiftly down the slate corridor, past the dining area to the front entrance of the castle. The Whistling Kites were gliding back and forth with the swings dangling from their feet.

"Sh-line up, arm's length from sh-each other," instructed Parlow. The children all lined up, bent their knees as the Whistling Kites slowly descended low enough for the swings to hit their bottoms. Quickly grabbing the ropes, the children were elevated up into the air. Wanjee turned back, looked down and shouted and waved with one hand back to Parlow, "Thank you, Parlow, I love you."

Parlow gave her a warm smile and quietly said to himself, "I love you too, child."

The Kites ascended higher and higher, over the Enchanted Sea World, over the water slide hill and continued North towards South Seabrooke island. The children had not seen this part of the island and were surprised at the vastness of land and bush that surrounded them below them. "How far is it from here?" shouted Tommy back to Wanjee.

"It's a very big island, my tribe live in the middle of the island, it will take 10 minutes flight time," Wanjee shouted back.

The children enjoyed the wind in their faces, their legs dangling below them and watching the dolphins play as they crossed over the ocean to South Seabrooke Island. After 5 minutes Wanjee called out, "There, look in the distance, that smoke signal is from my tribe," shouted an excited Wanjee.

In the distant sky were various sized smoke rings slowly rising then dissipating into thick lines of smoke drifting into the sky.

As the kites neared the smoke, the children could see the flickering of flames and a tribe of aboriginal people with their bodies painted, some only wearing a cloth around their waists. The sound of didgeridoos and singing could be heard and as the Kites began to ascend lower.

Wanjee could clearly see her parents waving and shouting, "Wanjee, Wanjee, Wanjee." Wanjee was so excited she wanted to jump off the swing in mid-air, her bottom was halfway off when the kite lowered her feet onto the ground, she jumped off running straight to her parents who ran towards her. They all embraced, jumping up and down and around in a circle.

Tommy, Jake and Maria jumped off their swings and the Kites flew away. They stood watching Wanjee and her parents and the excited tribe chanting and singing. "Wish I had a family like that," commented Jake.

"We do have a family like that, maybe not the humankind but we have our Enchanted Sea World family," replied Maria.

"You're right, they are pretty awesome," replied Jake.

"C'mon guys, come and meet my family," beckoned Wanjee to the others. After Wanjee introduced her family, the tribe began dancing, pulling Tommy, Jake and Maria into their dancing circle. They all began laughing and dancing around the large fire pit with all the painted bare bodies of the Muandik people. "C'mon guys, we will paint ourselves and dress up," said Wanjee.

It was a wonderful festive energy and the children were excited to paint their bodies. Tommy and Jake took off their shirts and several tribal people began wiping their clay tipped fingers over the boys' chests. Several tribal women painted Wanjee and Maria's faces, their arms and legs with white stripes and yellow dots until the children looked like part of the Muandik tribe.

The children copied the tribal dance and chanted the language to the sound of the didgeridoo until Wanjee's father gave out an enormous call. It was the call to eat. Everyone gathered around the fire pit. Tribal women served the children grilled fish with fresh fruit on large green palm leaves. The children looked at each other. The food looked delicious but there were no utensils to eat the food with.

Wanjee noticed her friends' confusion. "We eat with our hands," said Wanjee showing them how to eat with their hands. The others carefully copied her a little reluctant at first.

"You know, I think the food tastes better when you can feel it in your hands," stated Maria with a smile. The others laughed and agreed as they scooped their hands into the fish and into their mouths.

After the meal Wanjee's father stood up, the tribe kneeled before him. "Why are the tribe kneeling before your father?" questioned Jake.

"My parents are leaders of the tribe," replied Wanjee. Wanjee's father was a large gentleman, he had a commanding presence.

"I would like to welcome our daughter and her friends to this Corroboree celebration. It is rare to have non-indigenous people at our Corroboree but you are Wanjee's friends and we welcome you into our tribe," he concluded.

The sound of a didgeridoo began and the Muandik people began dancing, laughing and singing again. Wanjee danced with her mother and father as did Tommy, Jake and Maria. Wanjee tapped Maria on the shoulder and told her she was going to have some quiet time with her parents. She left her friends dancing with the tribe and walked with her parents to the quietness of the water's edge where they sat down on some large smooth-surfaced boulders together.

As Wanjee sat in between her parents, she rested her head gently on her mother's shoulder. They all sat gazing into the still water when Wanjee asked about her parents' health, "Are you fully recovered?" a hopeful Wanjee inquired.

"We have both recovered from influenza but we both have diabetes and must take conventional medicine," her mother replied.

"Can I stay with you now, my foster parents are horrible, they drink and don't care about me," said Wanjee pleading with her parents to come home.

"Wanjee," her father said in a gentle deep voice, "we know about your foster parents and we have made a report so we can bring you home, but, we are still recovering and by the end of your school year you can return to us. Parlow has agreed to allow you to visit every Friday after tutoring," her father concluded.

"But I don't want to go back to those horrible foster people," said Wanjee with tears in her eyes. Wanjee's father wrapped his arms around her pulling her close to him, "You will not go back to them, instead, we have spoken to Maria's father and arranged for you to stay with Maria until the end of the year," reassured her father.

"Oh thank you, I love you so much," replied Wanjee thankfully and wrapped her arms around both her parents.

"Hold on, how did you know about Parlow?" questioned Wanjee with curiosity.

"Parlow came to us, at first we were shocked to hear a talking Pelican but he explained your situation, and the Enchanted Sea world, we were sworn to secrecy," said her mother.

"Parlow and the Enchanted Sea World have been my family while you've been gone, I will miss them," replied Wanjee.

"No matter where or who your family are or how far away they are, they will always remain in here," said her mother with her hands gently resting on her heart.

They stood up and began making their way back to the Corrobboree, Wanjee ran up to Maria and Tommy who were dancing around with the tribal children. "Hey, did you know I'm coming to stay with you until the end of the term?" questioned Wanjee.

Maria looked pleasantly surprised, "No I didn't, but that is awesome," replied Maria. The two girls danced around in circles like fluttering butterfly's when Wanjee noticed Jake was gone.

"Do you know where Jake is?" asked Wanjee.

"Mmmm, no I don't," replied Maria. They began looking around.

Suddenly Wanjee pointed, "There he is, over next to my brother playing the didgeridoo." They all laughed and ran over to Jake who had been given some lessons by Wanjee's brother and was belting out an amazing melody of sounds.

"Wow Jake, you're a natural," commented Wanjee. Jake continued playing with a little smile on his pursed lips. The children suddenly heard the high pitch screech of the whistling kites over and above the deep bellowing sounds of the didgeridoo.

"Oh no, it's time to go, here come the kites," announced Wanjee. "I must say goodbye to my parents and the tribe," Wanjee said as she ran towards her parents.

Jake thanked Wanjee's brother for the lessons, gave back the didgeridoo and they all went over and thanked Wanjee's parents and the tribe for inviting them to their Corroboree.

The Kites circled the children with swings dangling from their legs. "We must line up," said Tommy.

Wanjee gave her parents one last hug, "See you next Friday, I love you," she said and ran over in line with her friends as the kites descended and swooped the children off their feet and into the sky.

Wanjee turned her head back shouting from above, "Bye, I love you," waving down to the tribe. The tribe gradually faded out of sight as the kites neared the Enchanted Sea World. The children could see Parlow waiting for them as the kites descended lower and lower until the children's feet touched the soft ground, they ran off the swings and the kites continued flying into the sky with empty swings dangling from their legs.

"Sh-hurry up," Parlow told them. "It's time to sh-go, we must sh-go straight to the tunnel," said Parlow.

The children walked at a fast pace with Parlow, all still painted in multi-shaded clay stripes and dots. As Wanjee walked she put her arm affectionately around Parlow's feathery warm, soft body, "Thank you, Parlow, for doing this for me, you have been my saviour and I love you," Maria said affectionately.

"Sh-you are very sh-welcome child," replied Parlow with an affectionate smile.

As the children neared the tunnel, Jake remembered they had forgotten their didgeridoos. "Hey, what about our didgeridoos?" questioned Jake.

"Sh-you can practice on them in the Enchanted SeaWorld, they are too big to take home," replied Parlow.

"That's okay, I know how to make one now, I'll make another one at home," replied Jake cheerfully.

The children arrived at the tunnel door and one by one were squirted up the tunnel by the whale's water from its blowhole.

By the time they landed back on Mangrove sands all the body paint had washed off. Tommy pulled the towel from around his waist and they all dried themselves and climbed on Parlow's back who ascended swiftly through the cool night air, dropping the boys home first. When he arrived at Maria's house, he told Wanjee she would stay the night with Maria. "But what about my bike and personal things?" questioned Wanjee concerned.

"Sh-you can collect them tomorrow, sh-your foster parents have been sh-taken away and put sh-into a Rehabilitation Centre," replied Parlow.

"That's a relief, they were horrible people," said Wanjee in a stern tone. "It was wrong of them to foster but they have help now so maybe they can change their lives. Everyone can change with the right care and support," Parlow said in his wise old voice. After Parlow had spoken Wanjee's anger towards her foster parents soon turned to pity, she hoped they could feel happy like her one day.

Chapter 10

Unexpected Connections

The following day, Wanjee got up early and walked to her foster parents' house to collect her bike and personal belongings. The house was empty beer bottles strewn over the floors, dirty dishes piled high in the sink and the odour of stale cigarettes lingered throughout the house.

Wanjee didn't know when or if her foster parents would return to their house but she left a note for them.

"To my Foster parents,
Thank you for letting me stay at your house.
I hope you can both find happiness as I have.
I wish you a happy, healthy life.
From Wanjee."

As she left the house, Wanjee heard a shrill bird call, it reminded her of the evil bird spirit dream time story. She quickly mounted her bike and sped away happy to never see that house ever again.

Instead of taking the main road, Wanjee decided to cut through the dense bush. Travelling like the speed of light she didn't see several large dugout bandicoot holes when the front tyre of her bike wedged itself into one of the holes catapulting Wanjee over the handlebars landing her in the scrub. Slowly standing and brushing dead leaves and grass off herself she heard a hissing sound behind her.

Turning around carefully, she saw a 6ft brown snake standing straight up looking at her, standing up like a walking stick with two beady eyes.

Without hesitation, Wanjee ran towards the main road leaving her bike in the bush. The snake went after her slithering and hissing behind her. Wanjee's feet hardly touched the ground. She was running faster than she had ever run, her heart was pumping so loud and fast she thought it would pop out of her mouth. Still, the snake pursued and still, Wanjee ran terrified the snake would catch up and give her a deadly bite.

Finally, she came to Maria's house, the front door was open, Wanjee flew over the stairs without touching a step, straight inside and slammed the door. Maria and her father were startled by the door slamming and ran to Wanjee who was sitting with her back against the door, sweating, puffing and shaking.

"What's wrong?" asked Maria concerned.

Wanjee could hardly get a word out of her breathless mouth except for, "Sn-a-ke, sn-a-ke."

Maria's father went straight out to the garden shed, grabbed a pitchfork and hessian sack. He crept around to the front verandah and saw a massive 6ft brown snake slithering and hissing up and down the front door. The snake saw him and began its pursuit towards him. Maria's father was ready, as soon as the snake was close enough he lunged the pitchfork down over the snake's head pinning it to the floorboards on the verandah.

He carefully grabbed either side of its spitting, hissing head and tossed it into the hessian sack, tying it with some hay band. "It's okay girls, you can come out, I got him now," called out Maria's father.

The two girls slowly opened the front door and cautiously appeared. "I don't know anyone that could outrun a browny, particularly a 6ft one," said Maria's father. "I was running pretty fast, even surprised myself," said Wanjee with a nervous giggle.

"Well I hope you'll run at the sports carnival next week, you will win all the races, which means our sports house has a good chance of winning," said Maria.

"Yes, I will be running, all I have to do is think about the brown snake chasing me and I'll burn holes in the running tracks." Wanjee laughed.

Maria's father told the girls he would deliver the snake to the island wildlife man. Wanjee asked him if he could pick up her bike and explained where she had left it in the bush.

After Maria's father left with the snake, the two girls went inside to have breakfast. As they sat eating toast and Vegemite with warm tea, Wanjee explained to Maria what had happened. "When I left the foster parents house, I heard a piercing bird screech, it reminded me of a dream time story about a spirit bird. I took a shortcut through the bush and the front tyre of my bike got wedged in a massive bandicoot hole flipping me over the handlebars and into the bush. That's when I heard the snake hissing behind me."

Wanjee was convinced the birds screeching had something to do with it all and explained the dream time story

160

to Maria. "The Muandik tribe tell of a story about a spirit bird when the giant Craitbul and his family looked for a place to settle in the South Eastern region to find peace. The family camped at Mount Muirhead and Mount Schank but were frightened away by the moaning voice of a bird spirit. The family moved to Mt Gambier and managed to escape from the spirit. They made an oven, but one day water emerged from below and extinguished the fire. They made four more fires and the same thing happened, the holes are now said to be the craters and lakes of Mount Gambier," concluded Wanjee.**(19)**

"Oh wow, maybe that was the spirit bird?" questioned Maria.

"Maybe," pondered Wanjee.

The girls decided to ride to Jake and Tommy's to tell them what had happened. On their way the girl's passed Miss Ellie's house, she was in her garden with her two Labradors, Stoner and Hoover who were laying in the driveway. The dogs were very friendly and soon got to their feet wagging their tails as they walked to the gate to say hello to the girls.

Miss Ellie slowly stood up with a smile, rubbing her back, wearing green gardening gloves and a wide-brimmed woven straw hat. "Hello girls, how are you?" inquired Miss Ellie cheerfully walking over to the girls.

"Fine, thank you," both girls replied.

"I haven't officially met you, where are you from?" Miss Ellie asked the girls.

"Well, I'm from the island," replied Maria.

"I'm from Kingston in South Australia," replied Wanjee.

"Kingston?" Miss Ellie replied excitedly. "I am from Kingston. My parents died when I was 8yrs old and I was fostered out to this island," replied Miss Ellie.

"Wow, that's amazing," said Wanjee excited at the connection.

"What is your mother's maiden name?" queried Miss Ellie.

"Watson," replied Wanjee.

"Not Irene Watson?" said Miss Ellie, even more excited.

"Yes it is," replied Wanjee with a giggle at Miss Ellie's excitement.

"Oh my goodness, your mother and I were best friends in primary school until they re-homed me. Look at this," said Miss Ellie pulling a silver necklace from under her shirt that had half a silver heart attached to it.

"Oh wow, my mother has a silver necklace with half a heart on it, she told me her best friend gave it to her before she left Kingston," said Wanjee, extremely excited and amazed.

"Please let her know we have met and hopefully, one day, she can come and visit me," said Miss Ellie.

"I will Miss Ellie, she will be very happy," said Wanjee.

The girls waved goodbye as miss Ellie walked back to her garden saying to her dogs, "Well, well, life is full of unexpected connections and surprises."

The girls met up with the boys and spent the day in the Pina Wali talking about the incident with the snake, the sports carnival next week and the connection between Miss Ellie and Wanjee's mother.

"You sure you want to run in the sports carnival next week?" Jake asked Wanjee in jest.

"Yep, I'm running," Wanjee replied with a determined tone.

"Well there goes our house's chance of winning the sports carnival." Jake laughed.

"C'mon, I'll race you home on the bikes, it's good training for next week," Jake said, although he knew full well Wanjee would beat him.

As Wanjee and Jake took off on their bikes, Maria and Tommy looked on with a smile. "Training for who?" Tommy laughed.

"Jake more like it." Maria laughed.

The next few days went by quickly, it was Wednesday evening and the children were preparing for the sports carnival, making headbands and finding clothes to match the colours of their sports house. Wanjee and Maria were in Moreton House which was yellow, Tommy was in Capalaba house which was red and Jake was in Redland House which was blue. Last year, Redlands house won the sports carnival but he wasn't too sure if they could retain the title this year with Wanjee running.

The following morning the children arrived at school dressed in red, yellow and blue matching their house colours. The entire school was buzzing with excitement, children chanting their house songs and carrying handmade banners of encouragement for their teams as the entire school assembled on the oval. Screams, chants, feet stomping, banners waving, applauds and roars of excitement from each house whenever they had a winning team member cross the line.

There were those who didn't like running or sports but were encouraged to compete, just participating meant more points for their house.

Girls and boys ran separately and in different age groups. Jake won several races as did Tommy, the scores were very close, only 5 points separating Wanjee and Jake's house. It was Wanjee's turn to race, she lined up next to all the other girls her age. When the gun went off so did Wanjee, all she could think about was the brown snake chasing her. She flew over the finish line with a breaking the school record. The timekeepers were astonished at Wanjee's time. "This isn't just a school record, it's a state record, maybe a national record," exclaimed the timekeeper.

Wanjee proudly went up to the records table and received her first ribbon congratulating the other runners on her way back to her house team.

After all the events had been run, it was now time for the school champion run to determine the fastest runner in the school. This meant boys and girls ran together. Both Jake and Wanjee had qualified with their times and lined up next to each other. "Our houses are on equal points," stated Jake.

"Yes I know, whoever wins, it's only a race and we will still be friends," Wanjee said.

Jake extended his hand shaking Wanjee's hand. "Friends," he replied with a smile.

Holding the starter gun, the time keeper extended his arm up into the air. "Ready, set" and "BANG" went the gun. Wanjee took off like a bullet, there was a whole day between her and the other runners. Wanjee crossed the finish line to the sounds of rhorkas cheers and shouts. "It's another record," exclaimed the timekeeper.

Jake crossed the line in second place, he was panting so hard he held his head between his legs. Wanjee walked over and patted him on the back. "Good run mate, I know how I'm going to be an ambassador and advocate for my culture now," Wanjee said proudly to Jake.

Still out of breath Jake had a giggle. "You realised this in a race?" he questioned her.

"Yes I did, I'm going to run for Australia," stated Wanjee with conviction.

"Wow, you could easily do that Wanjee, you have record-breaking times and you can outrun a browny," replied Jake admiring Wanjee's passion and skill.

The house points were tallied and Capalaba just beat Redland by two points. Wanjee was crowned School Champion' and awarded a trophy, a medal and record times that qualified her for the state championships.

Wanjee felt a sense of pride but more than that she felt a sense of contentment and confidence, Wanjee knew what she was good at now and would pursue her goal.

The following evening, Parlow picked Tommy and Jake up on time as always. When he landed on Maria's windows sill, the girls were ready, Wanjee took a spare bag so Maria could take some of Ibis chef's delicious food while she was visiting her parents.

The girls said the code of silence and floated onto Parlow's back behind Tommy and Jake. Once they arrived at the Enchanted Sea World Parlow reminded Wanjee she would be taken to her parents after the tutoring session. As they all walked up the glistening golden path Parlow turned and looked at Wanjee. "Sh-congratulations on your school Champion win," commented Parlow.

"Thank you, Parlow, I'm going to run for Australia one day," stated Wanjee with conviction.

"I believe you will, child," Palrow replied with a reassuring smile.

As they approached the castle, Wanjee wondered how Parlow had known about her win. "Hey Parlow, how did you know about my win?" questioned Wanjee.

Tommy began to laugh. "You know Parlow, he knows everything," he said. They all had a giggle and made their way into class, they noticed their didgeridoos still standing as they left them with brightly coloured symbolic art painted on them.

Wally emerged from the pool and up came the virtual whiteboard. This time when Dino appeared he was holding a sign, it read, "Congratulations, Wanjee School Champion." Dino slowly put the sign down and had a big smile, Tommy, Jake and Maria applauded Wanjee whose cheeks turned pink from blushing.

"I'm going to run for Australia one day," Wanjee said in a quiet voice.

"I can't wait to watch you," replied Dino.

The children chatted with Dino who told them he had passed all of his tests and was looking forward to the school holidays.

"Will you be coming back to the island for a visit?" asked Tommy.

"I would love to visit you but first I will spend some time with my mother and I have joined a marine biology junior camp, we are going to the Great Barrier reef for one week," Dino told his friends with excitement.

"Wow, that sounds awesome, you can stay at my place if you come over to the island for a visit, grandpa isn't going anywhere these holidays," gestured Tommy.

"That would be rad," replied Dino.

Wally instructed the children that chat time was up and learning must begin. The children said goodbye to Dino and began singing their times tables before spending time on some English, grammar and reading.

By now the children were fluent with their 12 times tables, Wanjee was reading fluently, Tommy and Maria were excelling in all subjects and Jake loved math and music.

Wally gave further instructions, "Put your pens down, you have all worked so hard you can practice playing your lovely didgeridoos."

"Yeah, yeah, awesome," the children all echoed and jumped out of their clamshell chairs, grabbing their didgeridoos. Jake was by now very confident at playing the didgeridoo. The others watched him and copied what he was doing, how he held his mouth, how he sat, and held the didgeridoo. There were lots of funny noises echoing in the classroom. Maria blew into her didgeridoo and nothing but saliva came out of her mouth like a dribbling baby, the others roared laughing, including Maria.

While the children were laughing Wanjee noticed a kite fly past the classroom window with a swing attached to its feet. Wanjee looked at Parlow who nodded his large protruding beak. "Yes."

Wanjee put her didgeridoo down and said goodbye to her friends. "I'll see you all soon, I'm going to visit my parents now," she said smiling.

"Say hello from us," said Maria.

"Have a safe flight," said Tommy.

"Tell your brother I'm getting better on the didgeridoo," said Jake.

"I will," replied Wanjee as she made her way to the castle entrance to prepare for the Kite who had begun descending.

Standing with bent knees Wanjee was swooped up into the sky across the Enchanted Sea World. As she peered below admiring the beauty of the crystal clear blue water and abundance of fresh fruit and greenery she thought it odd that Parlow had not come to see her leave. Never mind, she thought to herself, I guess he was busy. The Kite flew over the sparkling bay, Wanjee enjoyed the sites of passing albatross, seagulls and Ibis all searching for their seafood meal in the ocean. Flying North, Wanjee was now overlooking South Seabrooke Island and nearing her parents Muandik tribe.

As the kite began to descend, Wanjee could see her parents and the tribe waving. Then she noticed another large bird descending with them. When the bird came closer Wanjee was surprised to see it was Parlow, with Miss Ellie on his back.

"Hi Wanjee," Miss Ellie waved.

"Hi Miss Ellie," Wanjee waved back excitedly, thinking to herself how amazing it was that Parlow knew everything.

The Kite flew low enough to the ground for Wanjee to let go of the ropes and run onto the dirt as soon as her feet touched the ground while the Kite continued to soar back into the sky.

Wanjee's parents came running over hugging her when they noticed Parlow land with a stranger on his back. They stood in silence and watched as a strange woman climbed off Parlow's back and began walking slowly with a smile towards Wanjee's mother. It had been forty-five years since they had seen each other. Wanjee's mother looked confused but she felt there was something very familiar about this person.

Wanjee silently stood beside her parents with a big smile, knowing the story and waiting for her mother to recognise

Miss Ellie. Miss Ellie was only a few feet away from Wanjee's mother who still looked puzzled. Then Miss Ellie slowly pulled her silver half heart out from beneath her shirt. Wanjee's mother screeched and wrapped her arms around Miss Ellie and they both cried tears of joy.

"Oh, Ellie, Ellie, it's been years, look I still have my half heart," said Wanjee's mother pulling her silver necklace from beneath her shirt showing Miss Ellie.

"We have many years to catch up on," said Miss Ellie.

Miss Ellie and Wanjee's mother chatted over a delicious meal of crayfish, fresh berries and mixed fruit. Wanjee enjoyed listening to their childhood stories but sat there wondering how Parlow knew. "How did Parlow know about your friendship with my mother?" questioned Wanjee curiously.

"Ahhhh, we have our way of contacting each other," replied Miss Ellie with a cheeky smile. Wanjee realised that Miss Ellie must still have her medallion like Dino's.

Wanjee's mother invited Miss Ellie to stay a few days but Miss Ellie couldn't leave her dogs back on the island and agreed to stay a few more hours and return for regular visits.

The time had passed quickly with all the excitement when Wanjee noticed the Kite returning for her. "It's time for me to go but I will see you all next week," said Wanjee standing to hug her parents and get ready for the Kites descent.

"Wait here, Wanjee," said Wanjee's mother handing her a miniature bottle of oil for her epilepsy. "Thank you, Mother, I was almost out," said Wanjee attaching the miniature bottle to the chain around her neck.

Wanjee kissed her mother, bent her knees and within seconds was swooped up into the sky swinging beneath the Kite and waving to her parents below.

Meanwhile back in the Enchanted Sea World Tommy, Maria and Jake had just completed a delicious meal of mini potato pies, pecan pie and banana, strawberry smoothies. Maria wrapped several pieces of pecan pie in a palm leaf and squeezed it into her pocket.

After thanking Ibis for the meal the children made their way outside to wait for Wanjee. "Look," cried out Maria, "here comes, Wanjee."

The kite descended and as it neared the children Wanjee prepared to jump and run as soon as the Kite was low enough for her to touch her feet on the ground.

"Hey, how was it?" Maria yelled out, running after Wanjee.

"Oh it was fab and you'll never guess who was there," Wanjee replied.

"Who?" Maria excitedly asked.

"MISS ELLIE," replied Wanjee.

"How?" queried Maria.

"Miss Ellie contacted Parlow with her medallion and he flew her there," said Wanjee.

"Wow, your mum must have been surprised," commented Maria.

"They both cried tears of joy," replied Wanjee.

Parlow listened on with a sense of contentment, "Another successful surprise," he said with cheeky smile.

"C'mon children, I sh-must get you all home," said Parlow. Maria pulled the pecan pie out of her pocket and handed it to Wanjee.

"Can you put this in your bag otherwise it will get squashed?" she said.

"Oh yum," replied Wanjee peeking into the palm leaf and putting it into her bag.

The children lined up one after another as the whale squirted water out of his blowhole, rocketing the children one at a time up through the tunnel and onto Mangrove Sands.

Parlow was in a hurry as he still had to go back and pick up Miss Ellie from South Seabrooke Island. The girls waved goodbye to the boys. "WuWu (goodbye), see you tomorrow," they said.

After arriving at Maria's house, Maria said the code of silence and floated back into her bed. Before Wanjee said the code of silence she wrapped her arms around Parlow's feathery body. "Thank you for changing my life, Parlow," she said gratefully giving him a kiss on his long curved neck.

"Sh-you changed your own sh-life, I simply gave you the opportunity," replied Parlow with a smile. Once Wanjee had floated back into bed, Parlow flew off the window sill soaring high into the starlit sky.

Just as Wanjee was about to fall asleep, Maria quietly said, "When you return to your family, will you go to school there?"

"Yes, I'll return to my old school," replied Wanjee with a yawn.

"I'm going to miss you Wanjee, you are like a sister to me," said Maria with a little sadness in her voice.

"We will stay in touch and you can come and visit me," Wanjee assured Maria.

"Goodnight my best friend Wanjee."

"Goodnight my best friend Maria," they said to each other and fell fast asleep, toe to toe with contented smiles on their faces.

Chapter 11
Triumphs and Transitions

During the final weeks of the school year, Wanjee had started taking some of the islanders' dogs for walks to earn some pocket money. The walks turned into runs and became part of Wanjee's daily training routine for the State Championships. The children had regular jam sessions on their didgeridoos every Friday in the Enchanted Sea World and preparations had begun for the grade six graduation held every year in the recreation hall located near the ferry.

It was the last Thursday of the school year for the grade sixes, graduation was held in the evening. During the day parents and teachers carted prizes, certificates and decorations from the school to the recreation hall. The school was a buzz at this time of the year, students excited for the upcoming Christmas holidays and students transitioning from grade six to high school.

Maria and Tommy were excited to be graduating and invited Wanjee and Jake to attend. That evening as Wanjee helped Maria get ready plaiting her beautiful long blonde hair, Maria's father yelled out to the girls, "You both ready?"

Maria was surprised, "Wow, Dad is actually coming, he has never attended a breakup before," said Maria pleasantly surprised.

"Well, it is your final year at primary school, it is pretty special," said Wanjee with an affectionate smile.

"C'mon, I'm ready. Let's go," said Maria excitedly. Maria's father had dressed up for the occasion wearing his best white shirt and a blue satin tie.

"WOW! You look great, Dad," Maria said proudly.

"I only wear this outfit for special occasions," replied Maria's father.

As they drove to the recreation hall, they passed Jake riding his bike with a headlight attached to the handlebars. "Beat ya," Wanjee yelled out the window laughing as they drove past Jake.

Tommy was ready, his grandfather also decided to attend so Tommy was helping him get ready. His grandfather was so slow he wondered if they would ever make it on time. It was the first time his grandfather had attended anything. Tommy now recognised how difficult it was for his grandfather who had bad arthritis.

In the meantime, the hall had filled with parents, friends and students. The grade six students were instructed to take the front row seats, everyone else sat behind them. Maria took a front-row seat directly in front of Wanjee and her father. Jake raced down the aisle panting and sat next to Wanjee. "Beat you." Wanjee laughed.

"Oh derrr," Jake replied with a grin.

Maria turned around to Wanjee and Jake looking a little concerned. "Have you seen Tommy?" she asked.

"No, but he will be here," Jake assured her. Maria placed her jacket on the seat beside her so Tommy could sit there when he arrived.

The ceremony began with the Australian National Anthem. The principal congratulated all grade six students for completing their primary years and began announcing names in alphabetical order to come up on stage and receive their graduation certificate and a cute little signature stuffed bear with a graduation hat on its head.

Tommy's surname was Zimmick, he was always last to be called but Maria was starting to get concerned as they were halfway through the alphabet and there was still no sign of Tommy. Maria's surname was Wheelan, also at the end of the call-up. When Maria heard her name she walked up onto the stage shook hands with the principal and as she received her certificate and bear she saw Tommy with his arm under his grandfather's arm helping him walk, very slowly, down the aisle.

Tommy's grandfather couldn't afford a wheelchair so moving around was difficult for him. Maria had seen a wheelchair backstage where they kept the props, instead of returning to her seat she walked down the stage steps and around the back behind the curtains and came out pushing a wheelchair. Tommy smiled and suddenly the audience applauded loudly, not for the awards but for Maria. Maria's father was more than proud, he was honoured she was his daughter.

Grandpa sat in the wheelchair as Tommy raced up onto the stage to receive the final recipient of the grade six certificates. Maria wheeled grandpa down to the front next to where Tommy and she were sitting. Maria's father placed his hand gently on Maria's shoulder, leaned forward and whispered, "I'm so proud of you." Maria felt a glow of warmth in her heart she had never felt before from her father, it made her feel loved and very special.

Next on the agenda of ceremonies were the special awards for individual subjects. The principal had given out several prizes for sports achievements, one for social studies and then she announced the Math award. "This year we have two recipients of the mathematics excellence award. Both these students received equal final grades. This year the winners are Tommy Zimmick and Maria Wheelan."

Tommy and Maria high fived one another. Tommy's grandfather and Maria's father applauded loudly smiling and nodding to each other with pride. Both Tommy and Maria received a $50 gift voucher, a certificate and a trophy.

Just as they were about to leave the stage the principal told them to wait. "This is a unique situation, we also have two equal winners of the English literacy awards." Tommy and Maria looked at each other with a surprising smile. "This year the English Literacy award goes to Tommy and Maria." The applauds were deafening. Maria and Tommy proudly received another gift voucher, a lovely writing set, a certificate and a trophy. They made their way back to their seats, Jake and Wanjee high fiving them and admiring their trophies.

Tommy gave his awards to his grandfather to hold, it was the proudest moment of his grandfather's life. Maria gave her prizes to her father to hold, he too was equally overwhelmed with pride.

The principal instructed the two rows of grade six students to stand and turn to face the audience. They sang a farewell song they had practised for several weeks. A few of the grade sixes and some of the parents had tears in their eyes as they sang. There was massive applause when they finished singing the song.

The grade sixes took their seats and the principal spoke again. "Before we conclude this year's grade six graduation, I have one more prestigious award to present. This award is for the student who has the best overall achievements in all subjects. Last year, recipient of the *'Dux of the school award'* was Dino, you can see his name etched on the gold plaque hanging in the school administration building along with winners from previous years. This year we have two recipients of the Dux of the school award."

Everyone smiled, including Tommy and Maria. Wanjee and Jake were bursting to scream with excitement. "This year's Dux of the school award goes to," and the principal paused smiling and looking at Tommy and Maria, "yes, it goes to Tommy and Maria." Wanjee and Jake jumped out of their seats hugging their best friends, as did Maria's father. Tommy's grandad was helped out of the wheelchair and hugged his grandson.

Maria and Tommy walked back onto the stage to deafening applause, screams and shouts of 'Well Done', 'Yeah' and 'Awesome'. They both received a beautiful gold edged framed certificate that read, Dux of the School, and their names would be etched on the school plaque next to Dino's name.

The principal concluded the graduation ceremony with a closing statement. "Although awards do not define us as people, they are recognition for those who have worked hard to achieve their goals at the highest level. Those who reached their goals and worked hard, we are equally as proud of you.

Never ever stop trying and never ever give up on your goals or your dreams. We wish you all the very best as you make the transition from primary school to high school."

The hall erupted in applauding and cheering students. Students and parents dispersed congratulating the grade six students and signing their graduation bears. Wanjee and Jake quickly ran to Maria and Tommy with high fives and hugs, admiring their prestigious awards. "It's your turn for awards tomorrow," Maria told Wanjee and Jake, referring to the final school assembly for the year.

"That's tomorrow, let me sign your bear," replied Wanjee grabbing Marias's bear. She wrote:

> *"My sister, my best friend forever,*
> *follow your dreams,*
> *Love Wanjee xxxx"*

After the children signed the bears it was time to head home. Although Tommy and Maria were proud of their achievements they were humbled and honoured to be recognised for their hard work. Jake congratulated Tommy and Maria and headed home on his bike. "See you guys tomorrow in assembly," he said waving goodbye.

"See you tomorrow," the children yelled back then Tommy helped Grandpa into his car.

"Thanks, kids, this was the proudest night of my life," stated Grandpa.

The following day, Wanjee and Jake woke up early excited about their school assembly and final day of the school year. Maria and Tommy both slept in after their big night of celebrations.

Maria half-opened her weary eyes with a smile. "I'm leaving now, will you be coming to the assembly?" Wanjee asked Maria in a soft voice.

"I wouldn't miss it," replied Maria reassuringly.

Wanjee ran outside, jumped on her bright pink bike and sped off towards school. Today she decided she would let Jake beat her. Jake was also on his way to school. Wanjee could see him riding in front of her. He stopped at the crossroad and turned his head around to check for traffic he saw Wanjee behind him. "Beat ya," he called back to Wanjee, who smiled and bent over her handlebars to make it look like she was up for the challenge.

As soon as Jake crossed the road, he sped down the last 200 metres to the school gate. Wanjee was right on his tail when she pulled up next to Jake. "Well there you go, you finally won," Wanjee said slapping Jake on the back. They parked their bikes as the bell rang quickly making their way to class. Just as Jake was about to walk into the classroom he turned and faced Wanjee, "I know you let me beat you, there is no honour unless it is a fair race," he said with a smile. Wanjee smiled, a little embarrassed, and agreed to fair races from now on.

Maria had set her alarm and was on her way to meet Tommy, but when she arrived Tommy was still asleep. "GO and wake him," Grandad told Maria. She raced into Tommy's room shaking him.

"Wake up Tommy! Wake up! Or we'll miss the school assembly," Maria said loudly. Tommy sat up startled.

"Oh, dear. I've slept in," he replied quickly getting up. "Wait for me outside I'll be out in 5 minutes," he said in a panicked voice.

Meanwhile, the whole school had lined up ready to take their seats in an orderly fashion in the outdoor undercover area. Everyone was almost seated, grade fives were the last to sit down. "Hey have you seen Maria and Tommy?" Jake asked Wanjee.

"No, Maria was still in bed when I left but she promised to be here," replied Wanjee.

Nearly every grade five students had parents attend the assembly, all stood at the back of the seated students. Wanjee felt a little sad that her parents were unable to attend due to still recovering and Jake's grandad had been drinking the night before and still in bed with a hangover.

The assembly had begun and the principal had awarded certificates and awards from prep to grade four. It was now time for grade fives. Wanjee and Jake kept looking around for Tommy and Maria but still, there was no sign of them, making them feel a little disappointed.

The Principal announced the next award, "The next award is our mathematics award, this goes to" and just as the principal said "Jake Johnson," Maria and Tommy came tearing down the pavement on their bikes next to the outdoor assembly area yelling out, "Woohoo, go Jake." Jake proudly stood up, waved to his friends and received his award.

Maria and Tommy made their way to the back of the students already seated as the principal continued. "This year we have a new award for the most improved for all subjects and this year the award goes to Wanjee Watson." Wanjee couldn't believe it, she could hardly read before Wally tutored her. She stood proudly to the echoes of excited screams and applauds from Tommy, Maria and Jake.

"Finally, we announce next year's school and house captains, the school captain for next year is, Jake Johnson," announced the principal. More screams and shouts from his loyal friends. After announcing all the awards, the principal had one last award. School Sports Champion.

"This year it gives me great pleasure to award a very talented sportsperson who is leaving us, but we will definitely follow their sporting endeavours over the next few years. This year's school Sports Champion is Wanjee Watson," announced the principal holding a trophy with all the former school Sports Champions engraved on it, including Wanjee's name.

Wanjee was overwhelmed with pride as her friends cheered and congratulated her. The assembly concluded with excited students dispersing and mingling with their friends and parents. Another school year was over, it was time for holidays.

"Hey you guys let's go and get an ice cream, my shout, we should celebrate," said Maria to the others.

"Your shout? Who am I to say no?" Jake laughed. The children grabbed their bikes and headed to the shops. Wanjee had taken her dog-walking money with her before leaving Maria's house in the morning. When the children arrived at the shops, Wanjee told the others she needed to go to the chemist first, that she would meet them in the ice cream shop.

Wanjee wanted to buy Maria a gift before she left to go back to her family. The chemist had many lovely gifts. Wanjee looked carefully at sweet-smelling vanilla soaps, strawberry-scented body sprays, lip gloss, photo frames and then Wanjee noticed a small glass jewellery cabinet with earrings, watches and necklaces. There inside the cabinet, she saw a silver half heart necklace, just like Miss Ellie and her mother's, with a $7 label on it. Wanjee had $10 in her pocket. The shop assistant asked Wanjee if she needed help. "Yes please, I'd like that silver heart necklace please," replied Wanjee.

As she was standing at the counter, Wanjee noticed a bag of mixed jelly beans for $2, she paid for both items and put the necklace and change into her backpack, then hurried to the ice cream shop where her friends were still deciding what flavour they wanted. "What did you buy at the chemist?" questioned Maria.

"Oh I got us all some Jelly beans," replied Wanjee keeping her special present a secret.

Finally deciding on flavours, Jake selected chocolate, Tommy macadamia, Maria strawberry and Wanjee chose blueberry. The children sat on seats outside the shop enjoying their cold, creamy, melting ice creams and jelly beans.

The children were tired from the past two days of excitement and decided to all return home for sleep before Tommy, Maria and Wanjee's final night in the Enchanted Sea World together.

That evening Parlow arrived on Tommy's window sill, on time as always. As Tommy opened his window, Parlow smiled that cheeky smile when he was up to something. "I sh-have a surprise for everyone," he said with a cheeky wink.

"You're a big tease." Tommy laughed.

"That I sh-am son." Parlow laughed.

While Parlow was on his way to collect Jake, Wanjee was packing her belongings and awards into her backpack. Wanjee had written a thank you note that afternoon. "Would you give this thank you note to your father?" Wanjee asked Maria.

"Of course," replied Maria placing the note on her mantelpiece.

"I'll leave my bike here so I can ride it when I come back for a visit," stated Wanjee.

"Well, I doubt it would fit on Parlow's back." Maria laughed. The two girls giggled at the thought of it as they saw Parlow flying towards them in the moonlit sky. They quickly grabbed their ingots, opened the window and jumped into bed.

"Hello sh-girls, are you ready?" asked Parlow.

"Your last night," said Jake with enthusiasm, anticipating a forthcoming surprise.

The girls smiled, said the code of silence and floated onto Parlow's feathery white back behind Tommy and Jake. Tonight Wanjee went last as she had her backpack to carry. "What about my body?" queried Wanjee looking at herself in bed from Parlow's back.

"Do not sh-worry, your body sh-will not be visible once you return sh-home," replied Parlow.

As Parlow flew towards Mangrove Sands in the sparkling, starlit night sky the cool sea breeze swept over the children's faces. Wanjee felt excited to be going home but had a sadness in her heart to be leaving her best friends and the Enchanted Sea World family.

Parlow glided onto the soft white sand next to a large stingray hole and called the soldier crabs. Once they were all at the tunnel door, the children's rainbow serpent shined through. Today Tommy, Maria and Wanjee took their time, they closed their eyes and absorbed the coloured rays from the light on their skin feeling the warmth and appreciating every magical moment.

Jake watched the others feeling somewhat alone, his friends were all leaving. Parlow noticed Jake's mood and whispered in his ear, "Wanjee doesn't sh-know it yet, but I sh-will be picking her up sh-every Friday from her tribe to join you sh-in the Enchanted sea world sh-next year, but sh-it's a secret," he said with that cheeky wink of his. Jake immediately giggled at Parlow's pronunciation and immediately felt better.

As the children began walking up the golden glittering path, Cane flew past them squawking with excitement, the whales squirted water out of their blowholes, and the dolphins danced and splashed in the crystal clear water. The Enchanted Sea World creatures were definitely excited about something.

"What's going on?" Jake asked Cane.

"Squawk, Squawk, can't say," he replied flying towards the castle.

When they all arrived at the castle, a massive fire pit stacked with dry twigs and sticks had been made on the dirt 500mtres to the right of the castle. "Are we having a bonfire?" questioned Tommy.

"It's a surprise," winked Parlow with a cheeky smile.

"Oh Parlow," the children all said laughing.

The children were heightened with excitement, jumping and skipping as they made their way into the castle. To their surprise, coloured streamers hung from the pearl shell clad roof. Ibis chef was busy preparing the children's favourite party treats. Parlow was waiting for the children holding the red ruby door open as they looked at the streamers, intrigued by what Ibis chef might have been preparing in the kitchen.

The children's excitement was building they ran into their classroom. Inside were signs hanging all over the classroom that read:

Giving, Trustworthy, Respectful, Caring,
Honourable, Kind, Thoughtful, Helpful, Polite, Selfless,
Humble, Gracious, Truthful.

The children didn't quite understand what was going on. Wally, Delilah and Pedro slowly emerged from the water as Grython lay coiled up in the corner. "Take your seats, children," said Wally spluttering water from his large mouth. "Today th-is a very special day th-when transitions th-will be made. We congratulate th-you all on your fine achievements th-at school, you all worked so hard to achieve. BUT, awards th-and talent mean nothing th-if you are not a good person th-with them. Today, th-we celebrate th-and congratulate the fine human qualities th-you have all displayed, with th-and without th-your awards," concluded Wally.

The children now understood what all the signs meant, it made them feel very good. Parlow walked to the front of the class, "We have sh-three people leaving us today, Maria and Tommy before sh-you leave us for high school sh-you have earned your medallions," Parlow said, holding two medallions like Dino's. "First sh-you must relinquish sh-your ingots," he instructed.

Maria and Tommy smiled at one another, took off their ingots and walked up to Parlow who took their ingots and placed the medallions over their necks. Wanjee and Jake applauded their friends but Wanjee was a little bit sad that she had not earned a medallion as she would also be leaving. "Parlow, am I relinquishing my ingot?" questioned Wanjee.

Parlow gave her a cheeky smile, "No dear sh-you will keep yours sh-as I will be picking sh-you up from your tribe every Friday evening next sh-year before collecting Jake," announced Parlow.

"Woohoo," Wanjee and Jake jumped around high fiving each other.

"I knew you were coming back, Parlow told me the secret earlier," let on Jake.

"Oh your as bad as Parlow with secrets now." Wanjee laughed.

"Settle down sh-children," said Parlow with a smile. "I thought sh-we would celebrate our farewells sh-with a Corroboree today."

"Awesome!" The children heightened again with excitement.

"Can we play our didgeridoos?" questioned Jake.

"I hope sh-you all serenade sh-us with the sh-sounds of didgeridoos," replied Parlow.

"You can all go sh-and collect some coloured clay to decorate yourselves," instructed Parlow who had other plans. The children thanked their tutors for all their support and fun learning. "I will never forget you, Wally," said Maria stroking the side of Wally's wet bald head.

"Go and conquer th-the world, young lady," replied Wally with a wink.

The children made their way outside to their carts and headed towards the ocean shore to find their clay, waving at Johanna on the Ferris wheel and Mut and Tut on the water slide.

Meanwhile, while the children were busy finding clay, Parlow had disappeared, there was one more surprise he had planned for the children.

After the children had collected various shades of clay wrapped in palm leaves, they began to head back to the castle when Maria and Tommy veered up the hill beside the water slide. "Hey, where are you two going?" called out Jake.

"We're going to say goodbye to Ollie, Archie and the babies." Wanjee and Jake decided to wait at the bottom of the hill and let Maria and Tommy say goodbye together.

Once at the top of the hill, Maria and Tommy walked to the edge of the cliff where they could see Ollie's cave. They cupped their hands and called out, "Ollie. Ollie, Ollie," their voices echoing through the cave. Ollie, Archie and the babies appeared at the entrance of the cave waving up at Tommy and Maria.

Both Tommy and Maria cupped their hands again and yelled out, "Goodbye friends." The octopus all yelled back in unison, "Goodbye ph-friends," waving their tentacle arms. Tommy and Maria both felt a little heavy-hearted as they walked back to their carts and made their way back down the hill to Jake and Wanjee.

Wanjee noticed Tommy and Maria looking a little sad when they arrived back at the castle. Wanjee jumped out of her cart with her clay wrapped in palm leaves, "C'mon, time for some fun, let's paint ourselves," she said with enthusiasm. Tommy and Maria smiled, took their palm leaves of clay and they all began painting each other with dots and stripes on their faces, arms and legs around the bonfire.

When they had finished, they went back into the classroom to collect their didgeridoos. Strangely, Parlow was nowhere to be seen. Walking back outside with their didgeridoos Wanjee noticed Parlow flying towards them, she also noticed someone on his back.

"Look, here comes Parlow," shouted Wanjee pointing towards Parlow descending towards them.

Maria squealed out in excitement, "It's Dino, it's Dino." The boys were so excited they began high fiving each other and ran towards Parlow who had landed.

"Dino, Dino, how did Parlow manage to get you here?" an excited Tommy asked as he high fived his mate and gave him a hug.

"Parlow contacted me via the medallion and used your ingot to get me here," replied Dino. Both Jake and Maria gave Dino a hug and told him how they had missed him.

"Wow you've certainly grown taller," commented Maria.

"Yes, something I have no control over." Dino laughed.

Wanjee had not met Dino in person, she walked up to him, and extended her hand, "Wanjee," she said with a smile.

"Dino," he replied shaking Wanjee's hand.

"I like your body paint," commented Dino.

"C'mon everyone we have enough clay left over to paint Dino," said Wanjee pulling Dino by the hand toward the unlit fireplace.

A squawk came from above as Cane flew down and landed on Dino's shoulder, "I've missed you, my feathery friend," said Dino stroking Canes soft white feathers. Parlow watched with beaming pride at the joy on the children's faces and proud of who they were as people and the wonderful friendship they had formed with one another.

The children were giggling as they painted Dino. Tommy painted one of his legs, Jake painted the other leg while Maria and Wanjee painted Dino's arms and face. Wanjee stood back admiring their artwork on Dino. "There you go, all ready for a Corroboree," stated Wanjee. Dino noticed the Didgeridoos lying on the ground.

"Are these the didgeridoos you made?" he questioned picking one up and studying it.

"Yeah, Wanjee taught us how to make them, her brother taught me how to play," Jake said as he took the didgeridoo and began to blow into it making a melody of sounds.

Wanjee offered her didgeridoo to Dino who watched Jake playing and mimicked his technique producing a small sound. Tommy, Maria and Wanjee began to dance, "Hey, we need to light the fire," said Wanjee. She took two dry sticks off the top of the fire pit and found a bush of dry grass. Rubbing the two sticks fiercely into the dry grass again and again creating friction until a puff of smoke coming from the grass. She continued rubbing the sticks between her hands and blowing air onto the grass until the smoke finally turned into a flame. She carefully picked up the burning grass and placed it carefully under the large pile of sticks. The orange flames flickered and soon the sound of twigs crackled.

The children had watched in astonishment at Wanjee's fire-making skills.

"You're so clever, Wanjee," Maria commented.

"It is how we light fires in the bush," replied Wanjee. The burning flames had risen to a massive orange glow, Jake, Tommy and Dino played the didgeridoos, the sounds echoed throughout the Enchanted Sea World as Maria and Wanjee laughed and danced around the orange glow of fire.

One by one, the enchanted animals joined them and began dancing with them. Johanna twirled around with her scaly, grey tail swishing and thumping it from side to side, Mut and Tut did a rap bop with their little turtle heads, the whistling Kites swooped above in a circle, the dolphins, whales and Dugongs could be seen dancing, diving and playing in the water, even Parlow was tapping his feet on the ground.

Suddenly, the earth trembled beneath their feet, like an earthquake.

Large thudding sounds were approaching. "Look, here comes Toddalick," yelled Wanjee in excitement. Dino dropped his didgeridoo, standing open mouthed astonished at the size of the frog coming towards them.

"Who is Toddalick?" inquired Dino in astonishment.

"He is a magical frog related to a legendary aboriginal frog," replied Wanjee.

The Enchanted Sea World was buzzing with dancing creatures to the sounds of didgeridoos, painted, laughing children and a roaring fire. The food bell suddenly rang and Ibis chef flung open the castle doors pushing a trolley outside laden with an assortment of cupcakes, fruit salad, pies and the children's favourite drink. The children piled food onto palm leaves and sat around the fire.

"Oh I do miss your delicious food," commented Dino savouring every mouthful of potato pie. He couldn't resist having some pop fizz drink it had been so long and gulped several large mouthfuls. As Dino went to speak he burped a bubble onto Jake who was now en-captured within the bubble and began elevating above everyone, higher and higher with a mouth full of cupcake.

"Oh no we are not inside, he will float away," called out Maria concerned.

"Squawk, Squawk," Cane flew past the bubble popping it with his sharp beak but Jake had risen rather high and landed with his ankle twisted. He lay on the ground groaning in pain and holding his ankle. Toddalick thudded over to him and placed his gigantic pad over Jake's ankle. The children gathered around concerned for Jake. A penetrating bright glow shone from Toddalicks pad onto Jake's ankle and suddenly Jake felt no pain.

"Wow, that was amazing," commented Dino who felt bad about injuring his mate.

Just as Dino was apologising to Jake, Maria burped and a bubble landed on Tommy who began floating, this time Cane was ready and popped the bubble before it floated too high landing Tommy in the soft emerald green grass. The children could see that Cane was enjoying popping the bubbles so they all began burping bubbles onto each other. Cane was squawking and popping bubbles as the children dropped and rolled around laughing on the ground.

Wanjee stopped laughing when she noticed a whistling kite with a swing attached to its feet fly overhead. Instantly, her laughter turned to a sinking feeling in her heart. "I'm afraid it is time for me to go home," Wanjee announced.

"Oh no, it can't be that time already," replied Maria who also felt her heart sink.

"I must get my backpack," said Wanjee standing and brushing the grass off herself. She ran inside and grabbed her backpack, taking some sherbet bombs and cupcakes on the way out. The Kite had completed several circuits, it was time to say goodbye to her friends.

She walked up to Dino and shook his hand, "It was very nice to meet you, good luck with your studies." She faced Jake, gave him a high five and a firm hug, "Catch you next year, first Friday back, hey you'll beat everyone now," she said and they both laughed.

Wanjee then faced her best friend, "Can you walk with me a little bit?" she asked Maria pulling a small brown bag out of her backpack. The two girls walked away from the children and stood beneath a very large mango tree.

"My mum once said to me, sometimes in life you find that one true friend that is always there for you no matter where or how far away they are, they remain in your heart forever. You are my true friend, Maria and will always live in my heart," said Wanjee as she took the two half heart necklaces out of the bag.

"Oh, Wanjee, they are just like the hearts Miss Ellie and your mother have," said Maria hugging Wanjee with a tear in her eye.

There was not a dry eye in the Enchanted Sea World as the creatures and children looked on. Suddenly, Cram let out an enormous 'POP' and the stench and sound made everyone laugh. "That's definitely my cue to go." Wanjee laughed. She put her backpack over her shoulders and walked over to the emerald green grass bending her knees as the Whistling Kite descended and scooped her up onto the swing. "WuWu Wanggi," Wanjee called down to everyone.

"WuWu Wanggi," her friends and creatures called back waving.

Jake grabbed his didgeridoo and began playing the song he had written, the children all began to sing;

"Lonely nights I cried to sleep,
Until my friends, I did meet
Good food, Pina Wali time,
racing bikes, life is fine.

Mangrove Sands, Friday and you,
now I'm never ever blue.

Learning, driving, flying high,
one by one we say goodbye
Although we will soon part,
always together
in my heart.

Mangrove Sands, Friday and you,
now I'm never ever blue."

As Wanjee flew away to the sweet sound of her friend's voices and the melodic sounds of the didgeridoo, a colourful rainbow serpent appeared. It shone brightly, creating an arched pathway stretching from her friends standing below in the Enchanted Sea World, all the way to South Seabrooke Island. Wanjee knew they would always remain connected and that many more exciting and epic journeys lay ahead for all of them.

The End.

Consonants/Consonants and Consonant/vowel combinations
that the writer feels resembles each particular animal's sound.

Sh-	Parlow	Pelicans
Th-	Wally, Delilah, Pedro	Dugongs
Par-	Duff	Pufferfish
Poa-	Cram	Mud crab
Gr-	Mut & Tut	Turtle
Wh-	Cane	Cockatoo
Goo-	Joanna	Goanna
Ph-	Ibis Chef	Ibis
Ph-	Ollie, Archie	Octopus
Sc-	Grython	Python
Kar- S	hian	Whisteling Kite
Cr- T	oddalick	Green Frog